CW01626516

Blood AND White Roses

The Second in the Bethany Mortimer Series

REBEKAH FANNING

The Book Guild

First published in Great Britain in 2026 by
The Book Guild Ltd
Unit E2 Airfield Business Park,
Harrison Road, Market Harborough,
Leicestershire. LE16 7UL
Tel: 0116 2792299
www.bookguild.co.uk
Email: info@bookguild.co.uk

The manufacturer's authorised representative in the EU
for product safety is Authorised Rep Compliance Ltd,
71 Lower Baggot Street, Dublin D02 P593 Ireland (www.arccompliance.com)

Blood and White Roses is a work of fiction. The events portrayed
in it, while based on historical figures and interwoven with some
factual content, are the product of the author's imagination.

Typeset in 11pt Minion Pro

Printed and bound by CPI Group (UK) Ltd, Croydon, CR0 4YY

ISBN 978 1835743 836

British Library Cataloguing in Publication Data.
A catalogue record for this book is available from the British Library.

MIX
Paper | Supporting
responsible forestry
FSC® C013604

Blood and White Roses

Also by Rebekah Fanning

I would like to dedicate this book to my Ophthalmic Consultant, Elanor Turnbull, whose positivity and dedication to eye care gives me hope and inspires me to carry on writing.

Thank you Elanor, I appreciate you more than words can say.

Introduction

Here I sit once more at the high table adjacent to our glorious new king. Edward IV, King of England. The year is 1461 and I am no longer Bethany Mortimer of Stratfield Mortimer; I am now Lady Bethany Harsyck of South Acre. Wife to Pip, who is more formally known as Lord Philip Harsyck. Our marriage was celebrated quietly at the manor of South Acre shortly before the Battle of St Albans in 1455, in anticipation that if I were left alone, I would be financially provided for. Luckily, the worst did not happen, and our lord, Richard, Duke of York, was victorious.

Since then, bloodshed has destroyed our land and, alas, I fear that there is more to come. Tonight, as we sit here, hand in hand, we both know that our lives are about to change forever. For tomorrow, we travel our separate ways to avenge the deaths of the king's father, Richard, Duke of York; his brother, Edmund, Earl of Rutland; and his uncle, Richard Neville, Earl of Salisbury. All of whom were killed within the sight of Sandal Castle, at the Battle of Wakefield, a few short weeks ago.

This time, I travel not as a pilgrim, but as a fully fledged Yorkist spy. For there is deception everywhere and my mission is to infiltrate the households of those who are still loyal to the Lancastrian regime and to gather information. I feel a mixture of fear, anticipation and even excitement as I prepare to travel, but I am wary of the dangers. It is good then that – befitting my new status – I will no longer walk, but travel by cart with trusty Morris by my side. I will also be accompanied by Alard, Ned, Davy and Owain. Sadly, I must leave Pip, who has to remain to catalogue the dead from the recent battle at Towton. No doubt our paths will cross again along the way, but who knows where or when.

For now, I must rest, but tomorrow I will rejoin you and we will travel together from Towton Hall towards Warwick Castle and the household of the mighty Richard Neville, Earl of Warwick.

The Aftermath of Towton

As we pass the battlefield, I hesitantly look across at the fields, which have been churned by battle. Discarded possessions litter the ground. I can see broken pieces of armour and bloodied leather straps. Legs, arms and torsos are piled high and bear witness to the recent violence.

"Mind you keep your eyes in front of you, Mistress Bethany. You don't need to see any of this."

I turn to look at trusty Morris, whose eyes smile kindly. "We have a long way to travel, and I don't want you worrying the whole way. What is done is done. God bless the souls of the brave Yorkists who gave their lives for the king, and their dear departed lord, Richard, Duke of York."

With that, Morris crosses himself and I silently understand that he will speak no more of the battle. "Now, Mistress, as you know, we are on our way to Warwick Castle. A place that I know well from my youth. I used to scamper up and down the moat to the river and beyond, but that was when my legs were young." Morris chuckles to himself, and I can see from his face that he is remembering times past. I can also see that this is a good mechanism to avoid the horrors either side of the lane.

To my left, upon a hill, I can see a lone tree. *A yew tree*, I think. It reminds me of my childhood home in Stratfield Mortimer. Instantly, I recall my mother's face. Round and kindly. I struggle to remember her voice. Through my daydreams, I manage to hear her singing. An ancient song of love and union. Warmth floods over me and, before long, we arrive at our first stopping point.

Morris pulls gently on the reins and both horses come slowly to a halt. I have never seen such pretty horses. Both are chestnuts, with rich copper coats and dark brown manes. The only difference being that the one on the left, called Liege, has a big white face and the one on the right, called Freemantle, has four white socks.

"You see that church over there, Mistress? The one next to the manor house? That's called St Mary's. It's more of a chapel really – that's where we are going to pray for a safe deliverance."

I ponder on its beautiful simplicity. It is extremely small and rectangle in design, with a bell-cote at one end and a stone mullioned unglazed window at the other. The doorway, which sits towards the furthest end, by the bell-cote, appears to be made from various sections of carved stone. However, I am unable to make out any details at this distance.

Morris kindly takes my hand and helps me down from the cart. As I dismount, I catch sight of a group of men exiting the hostelry on our left. Without really looking, I know who they are – for one is playing raucously on a shawm and the others are bemoaning the noise.

"I hope that you're not going to play that for much longer. I have a cracking headache." As I turn, Alard, Owain, Davy and Ned all stand before me. I smile, and I'm glad of their company.

Alard, as gentlemanly as ever, steps forward and rubs his hands. "Mistress Bethany, here we are again, ready for another adventure."

A steeliness runs through my veins. "Yes, we have an important mission ahead of us."

All six of us look at each other with a mix of fear, trepidation and excitement. Ned, as usual, is more excited than anyone and starts playing his shawm once more.

Alard shakes his head. "Ned, will you please keep the noise down? I've already told you that I've got a cracking headache."

Smiling mischievously, Ned puts his shawm away, but I doubt that he will remain quiet for very long, as I really don't think that he knows how to. I chuckle quietly to myself.

Walking in a line, we make our way to the church door. Inside, hundreds of candles shine brightly, and there is an overwhelming smell of incense mixed with sweat. Men fresh from the battle pray earnestly for friends who have died. Their faces are etched with pain and stained with tears. Others have open wounds, which weep and bleed. Women of the parish go among them with pots of balm.

Finding a space, I kneel upon the cold stone floor to pray for a safe journey. Immediately, I begin to sob as I think of Richard, Duke of York, and the task at hand. I allow myself a little time to wallow in grief and despair, all the while knowing that such thoughts are fruitless. Time cannot be turned back, and no matter how many tears I shed, the reality is that he is dead, and there is nothing I can do to bring him back. However, by using my energies wisely, I can find the traitors who plotted his death and the downfall of the House of York.

Turning my attention back to the living, I now pray for those I am forced to leave behind at Towton Hall for safety. Alas, King Edward's reign is still new and hotly contested by the remaining Lancastrian Lords, who are still loyal to King Henry and Queen Margaret. Even worse, though, if King Edward's scouts are right, there is a traitor closer to home. One who appears loyal to the House of York, but is a turncoat, a charlatan, a wolf in sheep's clothing. Someone who masquerades in plain sight. Someone who must be rooted out and stopped. My tears have all dried now and, from somewhere deep within, I am filled with God's grace. For the first time, I feel like I will succeed. All I need to do is to watch, to learn and to listen, and to allow myself to become Lady Philip Harsyck of South Acre. For this will allow me to hide behind a façade. My ladies in waiting will be my armour and a clear mind will help me see events with more clarity. I pray again, and when I open my eyes, I realise that the sun must have moved position in the sky, as the weak rays of light are now coming in from a different angle. They bounce off the heavy stone memorials and a stone coffin, which lies nestled against the outer wall.

Rising, I bow before the altar and turn to leave. Outside, I stride to the cart with purpose and we head off for Pontefract Castle, where we will say goodbye to Richard, Duke of York, for ever.

Onwards to Pontefract and the Last Goodbye

Ned, obviously having forgotten all about Alard's headache, begins to sing. Unsurprisingly, it's a song about gambling and drinking. Wailing at the top of his voice, Ned recounts a tale of a young man's unrequited love, which is quickly followed by the oblivion of too much ale.

"That's enough of that, Ned," Alard announces sharply. "Apart from my headache, I don't think that's a very suitable tale for such a journey."

A laughing Ned agrees, "Yes, I expect you're right."

The landscape around here is extremely hilly, but this doesn't seem to faze either Liege or Freemantle, as neither are pulling on the reins, and Morris seems to be miles away in a daydream. Before long, we pass the old yew tree, which I first saw as we passed the battlefield. Snow still clings to the bottom of the trunk, and I shudder from both the cold and remembrances of the battlefield. I immediately force such images from my mind and look around me. For we are entering a small linear village, which has a surprisingly large parish church on the right-hand side of the lane, and a none-too-grand manor house on the left-hand side. In the churchyard, numerous bonfires smoulder and produce a large amount of choking grey smoke. I can see that deep trenches are being dug to the right of the church door, and that men are dragging large objects in hessian sacks and piling them high against the church wall. Horror fills me, as I notice that some of the sacks are oozing blood. Bile enters my mouth and I struggle to know what to do. Noticing my horror, Owain begins to sing gently and Morris pats my arm.

"Keep looking ahead, Mistress. This is a Lancastrian manor and those sacks hold the bodies of traitors. Shed no tears for them, for they are murderers."

Hearing that these people most probably fought against our dear lord at the Battle of Wakefield and our true king at Towton hardens my heart and anger wells up inside me. This is a very new experience, but one that I must learn to deal with. Indeed, I must learn to hide my feelings.

Grateful to leave Saxton, I stare directly in front of me and contemplate Pontefract and beyond. Alas, nothing good will come out of Pontefract and the most that we can hope for is warmth, good food and safety. For even though King Edward's household has recently taken up residence within Pontefract Castle, the town is still a hotbed of Lancastrian sympathisers.

Morris is the first to break the silence. "Ay, Mistress, we've only a few miles to travel now, and you'll be relieved to hear that we'll soon leave the hilly terrain behind us."

Laughing, Ned shouts out, "Not as glad as Davy, Owain and me, though! My blisters are getting worse with each step. Heaven knows why Alard makes us walk. We could guard the cart just as easily from the inside."

Alard responds plainly, "Now, Ned, you know that's not true. How on earth could you prepare to shoot arrows when being shaken around in the back of the cart? To my mind, you're getting soft."

Sensing an opportunity to cause mischief, Morris joins in, "There's nothing wrong with my driving. The cart is as steady as a rock and the boys upfront are being as good as gold."

Leaning over, Morris whispers in my ear, "It's like the old days with Alice. She never could work out when I was pulling her leg either."

Smiling, I sit back and remember my first adventure away from home. I wonder where Alice is now. "Morris, do you ever see Alice?"

"Yes, Mistress, she's older now and rarely travels with the baggage trains, but I see her a couple of times a year when I lodge at Fotheringhay Castle."

My heart leaps with joy and an abundance of questions follow. "Is she there now? We're going to Fotheringhay Castle, aren't we? Will I see her?"

"Oh yes, Mistress, you'll see her, but you'll probably hear her first. As loud as ever, that one." Morris laughs energetically.

The light is beginning to fade as we enter the wooded area, which leads to the stone bridge crossing the River Aire. Even from this distance, I can hear the noise of the deep rushing water. Danger must lurk close by, as Morris has slowed the horses to the equivalent of a crawl, and Alard has jumped down to guard the front of the cart with Ned, while Davy and Owain guard the back. All have drawn their blades and I notice that even Morris has a blade beneath the sheepskin that he sits upon. Pip's words ring in my ears and

I am glad now that I listened to his concerns before I left Towton Hall. I gently pat the little knife, which sits within a concealed pocket in my outer kirtle.

Luckily, no blades are needed and as we emerge from the wooded area, I catch my breath, for ahead of us I can see the mighty Pontefract Castle in the distance. Sitting proud on a huge mound, heavy stone towers nestle for protection within a solid stone curtain wall. I cross myself, as I think of our late King Richard II, who was held hostage within the castle and eventually starved to death. The castle looks impregnable from the outside, but equally I imagine that it appears a daunting prison from the inside. I ponder on how my ancestor, Roger de Mortimer 4th Earl of March, must have felt as heir presumptive to King Richard II. Was he frightened? Did he fear imprisonment and death? Or did he bravely pursue his birth right? Alas, I fear that most of my family's history has been lost in the mists of time.

As we draw closer to the castle, we turn sharply to the right and head towards the drawbridge. The road becomes bumpy and I can see that Liege is becoming agitated. He is swishing his tale and nodding.

Morris gently pulls on the reins and calls out to him, "Come on, Liege, my boy, don't play up now." Morris's words seem to calm him. "Sorry, Mistress Bethany, Liege always plays up when there are cobbles to navigate. He remembers, you see. He's the bright one; Freemantle just plods along, but Liege thinks too much." Morris chuckles.

Pontefract Castle is even more impressive close up, but I feel only sadness. For inside are the dead bodies of our late lord, Richard, Duke of York; his son, Edmund, Earl of Rutland; his brother-in-law, Richard Neville, Earl of

Salisbury; and his nephew, Thomas Neville. I bite my lower lip as hard as possible as we pass under the heavy portcullis, for I must be strong and not cry in public.

Inside, we are greeted by a very tall, thin man, who is wearing the most magnificent green velvet robes. He has ermine at both his neck and cuffs. Surprised at such extravagance, I am unsure how to proceed. Looking around me, I notice that there are numerous metal torches attached to the heavy stone walls, all of which burn brightly and spit fire into the air. It is at this point that I realise that we are not alone. Morris leans over and whispers in my ear.

"Mistress, please remain seated. I sense that your welcoming party has arranged a set of dismounting steps for you. As Lady Philip Harsyck, this sort of reception befits your position. My advice is to remain dignified and confident at all times. For if there is a traitor at large, you'll need to keep all your wits about you. As always, trust no one but us."

I smile and pat Morris gently on the hand.

Owain steps forward and offers me his hand. "Lady Harsyck, please let me help you."

I take Owain's hand and climb down from the cart. It feels strange to be called Lady Harsyck by my friends, but I know that it is necessary if I am to assume my disguise. Standing straight, I smooth my new pale-blue woollen kirtle. It is of far grander quality than I am accustomed to, and it's much warmer than my old linen one. The wool is soft and the creases fall away easily. Before I move forward to greet the man in green velvet, I push back my matching cloak, so that I can shake his hand.

"Good evening, Lady Harsyck. I am John of Methley, the Steward of Pontefract Castle. I have seen to it myself that your room has been prepared to the highest possible standards."

With this, John claps his hands loudly and from the gloom, a rather timid young woman approaches and curtsies low. The fabric of her kirtle is almost as fine as mine and her coif is as white as snow. When she smiles, her eyes light up and dance.

"Lady Harsyck, please let me introduce you to your new lady-in-waiting, Ursula de Clare."

We smile graciously at each other, before John of Methley breaks the silence. "Lady Harsyck, if you would like to follow me, I will take you to the great hall."

Almost immediately, I feel repelled at being inside the castle. "That is most kind of you, John, but I would prefer to be taken to my room."

"Why, of course, Lady Harsyck, but food has been laid out for you in the hall."

"Again, that is very kind of you, but I would prefer to dine alone, on a plate of fresh bread and a jug of watered wine."

With this, John instructs Ursula to collect my refreshments and we head off towards my room.

As we near the top of the stairs, I feel an icy blast of air from an un-shuttered window. I begin to tremble and shake. I do hope that my room has a lit fire within it. As John opens the door, I realise that I was foolish to worry, for the room is impeccably decorated and a cloud of heat greets me.

"I will leave you here, Lady Harsyck. Ursula will not be long."

I thank John and close the door quickly behind me. Bolting it firmly, I look around and shudder, for – in spite of all its beauty– I do not like this place at all. There is a feeling of doom and death in the air.

Startled by a knock at the door so soon after John's departure, I call out, "Who's there?"

"It's me, Lady Harsyck, Ursula. I have your bread and wine."

"Thank you, Ursula, please leave it by the threshold. I will collect it shortly."

"But Lady Harsyck, I am here to serve you. Would you deny me entry to your room?"

"Thank you for your kind offer, Ursula, but I would prefer to eat alone and rest tonight. Today has been draining and I am not in the mood for company."

"Of course, my dear lady, I will see you when we break our fast tomorrow."

Immediately, I can hear the sadness in Ursula's voice and my heart feels heavy. I must, however, test her loyalty. If she is good and true, she will soon regain her cheerful demeanour, but if not, I will know that her countenance is false.

I remove my cloak and carefully lay it across a beautifully carved wooden chair, before taking off my coif and letting my hair tumble down. Sitting on the edge of the bed, I unbuckle my boots and kick them gently to one side. The mattress feels soft and I lie down.

I awake to birdsong and realise that I must have fallen asleep as soon as my head hit the pillow. I rise and shake my head, as if to blow the cobwebs away. There is a knock at the door.

"Lady Harsyck, are you well? I notice that your plate is untouched." Ursula's voice is soft and gentle, and I can hear genuine concern in her voice.

I immediately go to the door and unbolt it. "Oh, Ursula, I am so sorry. I must have fallen asleep immediately."

Ursula smiles as she looks me up and down. I become acutely aware of my crumpled kirtle and my messy hair. "I will fetch fresh refreshments for you and inform Owain that you are awake. He would like to deliver your wooden chest."

"Thank you, Ursula. I could do with a change of clothes and something to eat and drink."

With this, Ursula turns and walks away.

As always, I am pleased to see Owain and I have a long list of questions to ask him: "How is everyone this morning? Did you all sleep in the great hall? Are the horses rested? What time are we leaving?"

Owain laughs. "I can see that you are eager to leave already. So are we. We had a ghastly night. There was no room in the great hall, so we all had to sleep with Liege and Freemantle in the stable block, and if that wasn't bad enough, Ned drank too much wine and played that awful shawm well into the early hours. Alard is not happy."

Before I can reply, Ursula returns with a plate of pandemain and brie. Noting Owain's expression of longing, I offer to share.

"Thank you, Lady Harsyck, but I will break my fast with the others in the stable block."

After breaking my fast, I undress and sit on the edge of the bed, while Ursula prepares my clothes for the day. Sadness fills my heart, for a new dark-brown woollen kirtle awaits me.

"Lady Harsyck, would you be kind enough to stand?"

On standing, I notice that Ursula's eyes are moist and that her face is etched with pain.

"Ursula are you crying?"

"Yes, Lady Harsyck. Please forgive me, but I cannot shake the thought of Edmund, Earl of Rutland, lying cold and headless in the chapel."

In this moment, I can see that Ursula is trustworthy. Crossing ourselves, I attempt to get to know Ursula a little. "Did you know the Earl of Rutland?"

"No, not really, but I met him on many occasions at Fotheringhay Castle and beyond. We used to exchange glances and he would wink at me when no one was looking, and on St Valentine's Day last, he danced with me." Ursula smiles. "He was so handsome, with soft blond hair and beautifully kind eyes."

Realising that a shared grief unites us, I invite Ursula to call me Mistress Bethany when we are alone and in private.

"Thank you, Mistress Bethany, that is most kind of you."

Now dressed from head to foot in dark-brown wool, Ursula helps me into my new shoes. The leather is tight and painful; however, I know that it will soften in time. Last of all, Ursula covers my hair with a matching dark-brown linen coif and, at last, I am ready.

"Mistress, I will fetch Owain and Davy to accompany us to the chapel."

Unable to speak, I nod and wait patiently. On their arrival, I attempt to stand, but my legs fail me and I fall backwards onto the mattress.

Ursula screams, "Mistress, what's happening?!"

Owain, much more level-headed, realises that it's the shock of what lies ahead that is paralysing me. "Lady Harsyck, please let me help you."

With this, Owain outstretches both of his arms and I use them to lift myself. For a split second, my mind returns to Newmarket and both the terror of being attacked and Owain's gentleness when looking after me.

"Thank you, Owain. Shall we go while I can still stand?"

A smiling Owain nods and leads the way.

The outside air is even colder than before and a thin layer of frost clings to all the roofs. As we approach the entrance of the chapel, I notice that it is guarded by two men at arms in the livery of King Edward. Standing either side of the door, with their swords unsheathed, they appear ready for combat. Davy, having gone on slightly ahead of us, has paved the way for our smooth entry and now begins the formal introductions.

"Lady Harsyck, please let me introduce you to Peter of Pontefract and Simon of Sandal."

Both bow their heads respectfully and I sense from their faces that they recognise my title.

Peter is the first to speak. "Aye, Lady Harsyck, I am pleased to meet you. Your reputation goes before you."

I smile and thank Peter for his kind words.

Before I enter the chapel, I pull my hood up over my coif and wrap my cloak tightly around myself.

Owain steps forward and whispers in my ear. "As planned, we will leave you here, so that you can enter the chapel and mourn alone, but do not fear, we will be here should you need us. Lastly, please do not be alarmed, for inside there are four Franciscan monks who pray continuously for the souls of our lord, Richard, Duke of York, and his son, Edmund, Earl of Rutland."

I look at Owain and begin to question him. "Do they lie alone, or are they joined by Richard Neville, Earl of Salisbury, and his son, Sir Thomas Neville?"

"No, they lie alone. Richard Neville and his son lie in another part of the castle. It was deemed far too dangerous to house all of the bodies together."

I begin to shake violently, as I imagine their heads being taken down from Micklegate Bar in York, before being reunited with their newly exhumed bodies.

Owain, noticing my shaking, looks concerned. "I can accompany you inside if you'd prefer?"

"Thank you, Owain, but this is something that I must do alone."

With this, Owain nods towards Simon of Sandal, who slowly opens the chapel door just enough for me to enter and then closes it quickly behind me. Inside, it takes quite a while for my eyes to adjust and, once they do, I struggle to breathe. Gasping for air, I begin to sob uncontrollably, as I notice that both coffins lay side by side directly in front of me. Duke Richard on the left and Edmund on the right. Both are draped in heavy crimson velvet, which has been embroidered with seed pearls and edged with ermine. The only difference being a small golden crown, which sits at the head of Duke Richard's coffin.

Falling to my knees, I cannot control my grief any longer. Tears flood from my eyes and soak the neckline of my kirtle. I hear myself cry out, "Richard, oh, Richard, why did they do this to you? Why did they kill you and mutilate your body? You, the rightful King of England. A man of honour who sought only to protect the weak and to meter out justice in a good and true manner." I immediately choke and answer my own question. "They killed you because you are a Mortimer and a man of honour."

The floor is cold and I immediately remember lying prostrate before the altar on the church floor before I left home to go on pilgrimage to Walsingham. My mind then flits between thoughts of Duke Richard masquerading as

Roger and our meeting many years later at Bodney, when Duke Richard's true identity was disclosed to me. Through the tears, my heart is light as I remember his smile and his hands holding mine. Anger then bubbles up inside my stomach.

"Do not fear, Richard, for I will find the spies that linger within King Edward's household. I will unmask their treachery, and I will seek retribution for yours and Edmund's deaths." I then clasp my hands together tightly in prayer. "Dear Lord, I beg that you give me the strength to seek out the evildoers, and the ability to see through the fog of deception that surrounds these deadly deeds. Lord, I beg that you be by my side and guide me wisely."

Lying on the cold floor, I continue to sob until I feel a warm hand gently touch my head. Startled, I look up and see a kindly monk standing over me.

"Lady Harsyck, please forgive me. I did not mean to startle you. Please let me help you up. I fear that the cold will seep into your bones."

Gratefully, I wipe the tears from my face with the sleeve of my kirtle and accept the monk's hand. Standing, I bow my head and apologise. "Brother, please forgive me. I should not have cried aloud or broken the peace of this chapel."

"Why, my dear, you have nothing to apologise for. I have also shed many tears while praying. I also feel the same anger at Duke Richard's and Edmund's deaths. For I have known both for many years. Come, let's go and sit on those chairs over there."

Following the brother, we retreat to the corner of the chapel closest to the golden crown. From this angle, I can see a small solitary sapphire surrounded by pearls and many finely enamelled white roses. Once more, tears begin to stream from my eyes and I am unable to control them. With this, the kindly brother hands me a square of white linen and begins to introduce himself.

"Lady Harsyck, please permit me to tell you a little of my life. I am Brother Pendlebury, a Franciscan monk, and a member of the Order of the Friars Minor. I follow the teachings of St Francis of Assisi, and it is through my devotions that I met Duke Richard many years ago." With this, Brother Pendlebury crosses himself. "Duke Richard was closely associated with the Friars Minor and was a deeply spiritual man. A rarity among many of his peers. Did you know that on his travels he was accompanied by a portable altar from the Holy Land, so that he could say his prayers and hear mass before sunrise wherever he was?"

"Alas, Brother, I know very little of Duke Richard's life, only that as a Mortimer we were distantly related."

Brother Pendlebury smiles as I recount how I knew Duke Richard as Roger when I was growing up.

"What a beautiful memory. I would say that's one to cherish." With this, Brother Pendlebury stands and takes both of my hands. "Lady Harsyck, shall we leave the chapel now? Owain informs me that you are set for Sandal Castle."

Sadly, I nod my acceptance of the situation and try to stand, but my legs are so weak that I have to sit down again immediately. The enormity of knowing that I will never be in Richard's presence again overwhelms me. However, after a few minutes of composing myself, I suddenly feel an urge to touch Richard's coffin. This time, my legs feel strong. I stand and walk with purpose to the foot of Richard's coffin. Silently, and without being seen, I part the crimson velvet drape and place a small wooden cross gently into Richard's coffin. To cover any noise, I cough and shuffle my feet. Looking up, I can see that Brother Pendlebury is oblivious to my actions. I just hope that no one removes it before Richard is buried and that it remains with him.

Sandal Castle Awaits

Leaving the chapel, I am grateful to see that Morris is sitting aboard the cart waiting for me. I take his outstretched hand and climb aboard. Sitting at the front, next to Morris, I ask when we are due to leave.

"The others are on their way, Mistress Bethany. We'll be on our way shortly." Morris, noting my tear-stained face, gently pats my hand. "Tis a sad day indeed."

With this, I realise that Morris has also been crying and that his eyes also shine with tears. In turn, I squeeze his hand and we sit in silence.

The silence, however, is broken by Ned who has taken charge of loading my wooden chest onto the back of the cart. "There's enough room for Ursula, but we'll all have to walk."

Alard, still apparently annoyed from his night in the stable block, calls out, "Ned, that was the plan or had you forgotten in your drunken haze?"

"No, Alard, I remember. I'm just making sure that everyone knows what's happening. That's all."

Morris leans close and whispers in my ear, "I reckon that we'll all be glad to leave this place. They've done nothing but swipe at each other since they paid their respects in the chapel this morning."

In no time at all, everything is securely packed and Ursula climbs aboard. Squeezing herself between various sacks, Morris calls out, "It's time to leave now, but before we go, let's say one last goodbye to Duke Richard and the young Earl Edmund."

Lowering our heads and crossing ourselves, we all say our silent goodbyes, before Liege and Freemantle take up the reins and slowly move away.

To my mind, Pontefract appears a very pleasant town. The long high street is thronging with people going about their business in a frenetic way. It appears that no one wishes to loiter, as there are no groups or individuals standing around. I shudder as I imagine how frightening it must have been when the Lancastrians soldiers stormed their town. I cross myself and say a silent prayer for all those who are loyal to King Edward and his family.

As we leave via the south gate, I notice the entrance to a cave. Inside, a hermit sits upon a large chunk of rock surrounded by a huge crowd. He is chanting loudly and blessing people before they enter through the gate. Akin to a gatekeeper, he collects coins and bread from the travellers. Even from this distance, I can see that he passes the coins to an accomplice, presumably for safe-keeping, and he puts the bread into numerous baskets that surround him. From the look of it, the poor of Pontefract will not go hungry today. I ask Morris if we can stop, as I would like to donate a coin or two for the poor of the parish.

"Sorry, Mistress Bethany, we can't stop here. It's not safe. See those tatty soldiers over there. The ones with the blood-soaked livery of John Clifford. They may well be the out-of-control savages who slaughtered young Earl Edmund."

Immediately, I can feel my blood boil and I want to scream at the top of my voice and run them through with the small blade that hangs at my waist. How dare they mingle with the poor and how dare they be blessed! They deserve no mercy.

Morris, seeking to calm me, nudges me none too gently. "Mistress, we all feel the same way, but our mission is to hunt down the traitors at the very top – those who may well be planning the ambush and slaughter of King Edward and his family. Silence is needed. They are just the foul dogs who took their orders and did the deed. Anyway, there are only seven of us, and who knows how many more of those are concealed close by?"

Knowing Morris to be right, I retreat within my hood and cape. Sitting motionless, I consider how I am going to hunt down and identify the traitors.

My red-hot anger soon passes and everyone's mood is lightened by Ned, who has produced his shawm and is now playing loudly. However much it hurts to move on, move on we must. Lowering my hood, I look around at the beautiful scenery. Birds soar high above the rolling hills and sticky green buds adorn tree after tree. I remember the harshness of the winter just gone, and I long for summer. Feeling warm, I undo my cloak and push it from my shoulders.

"Now, Mistress Bethany, please be careful. You don't want to catch a chill."

For the first time in days, I allow myself to relax and breathe. The weak sunshine washes over me and I am glad to be alive. "Again, Morris, you are right."

"Yes, I know," Morris replies. "I'm always right."

Ursula chuckles.

Ned, becoming ever more raucous, begins to dance a merry jig and, to everyone's surprise, Alard joins in. Grateful that they have made amends, the mood of everyone improves. The hours pass by and we eat on the move. Davy, having thought ahead and procured supplies in Pontefract, has caused a great deal of excitement by handing out turnip pasties. How I love it when the turnips have been mashed and spiced with black pepper. My hunger is such that I even eat the outer rim of the pastry – it may be a little burnt, but it still tastes good to me.

Ned, as mischievous as ever, calls out, "I think we all need a drink now. Ursula, if you would be so kind as to delve into the sack next to you, you'll find an extremely large leather pouch at the bottom. This holds the finest ale that money can buy. You'll also find a collection of wooden beakers. May it never be said that I don't think of others."

Laugher fills the air, as this is obviously a jibe at Alard and the events of the stable block.

In what seems like no time at all, we draw to a halt at the end of a long drive. Morris turns and announces that we are nearing Sharlston Hall, but we must wait for our scouts before venturing any further.

With this, Ursula becomes animated and moves closer. Whispering in my ear, I can hear and sense her sadness. "Mistress Bethany, Sharlston Hall is a fine place and one that holds a very special place in my heart, for this is where I used to catch a glimpse of Earl Edmund when he visited on official business."

As Ursula moves her head away, I can see that she is crying again. I stand, reach out my hand and gently take hold of hers. I can feel her tremble and I seek to comfort her before Morris asks us both to sit. Taking up the reins of Liege and Fremantle, we move forward.

"I'm so sorry, Mistress Bethany, but Alard has made the sign to advance and we must not keep him waiting. Sharlston Hall is not safe. There has been much intrigue here within the last three years. Home to the poorer and more volatile branch of the Neville family, John Neville, the late Baron Neville de Raby, was a turncoat of the very worst kind. Not only did he constantly taunt and make difficulties for Richard, Earl of Salisbury, in life, he sided with Queen Margaret and then cruelly deceived Duke Richard." Morris crosses himself and goes silent.

Unaccustomed to such behaviour from Morris, I beg for more information.

"Please forgive me, Mistress Bethany. I cannot contain my emotions."

Morris begins to gasp and I fear for his health. Unsure of what to do, I look around and see Owain surrounded by soldiers in pale blue and white livery. They are arranging themselves into a line and preventing access either into or out of the driveway.

"Please, Mistress, do not tell Owain or the others. I am old and they may choose to retire me."

"But, Morris, I am frightened. You cannot breathe."

I notice that Ursula is frantically rummaging through her satchel and seemingly searching for something. To have them both acting strangely is very disconcerting. Almost immediately, Ursula stops her rummaging and unsteadily gets to her feet and passes me a large lozenge.

"Here, Mistress, this will help Morris breathe."

I look at the lozenge with suspicion before Ursula explains that she made it herself with crushed garlic, onions, rosemary, thyme, cumin seeds and honey.

"They taste vile, but my family have sworn by them for years. I always travel with a few in my bag for emergencies."

Morris nods gratefully, before accepting the lozenge. After placing it in his mouth, his face immediately begins to contort with disgust.

Ursula, now sitting directly behind us, apologises. "I'm so sorry, Morris, but I did say that they were vile, didn't I?"

Morris bravely nods and continues to suck the vile lozenge as we travel down the long drive in the direction of Alard.

Drawing the horses to a halt, it is obvious that the lozenge has worked and that Morris can breathe normally once more. Miraculously, he is able to call out to Alard in his normal way. "Eye lad, we need to be quick. I want to get away from this place as soon as possible."

To this, Alard agrees. "Yes, Morris, that's the plan. Davy and Ned are inside as we speak. They are gathering together all of the rolls and the parchments that they can find. The household is subdued at present, but violence could erupt at any moment." Alard, turning to face both myself and Ursula, kindly, but firmly, asks us both to stay put and not to leave the cart. "Please be prepared to take the rolls and parchments from Davy and Ned as quickly as possible and to place them carefully into an empty dry sack. The information that they contain will be highly valuable in King Edward's struggle against Queen Margaret and the other traitors."

Shocked at Alard's obvious state of tension, I hitch up my kirtles and carefully climb into the back of the cart, ready to help Ursula when the time comes. As soon as Alard steps aside, I gaze upon Sharlston Hall in all its glory and contemplate what I have just heard. The hall looks exceptionally fine and, from what I can see, consists of one linear building, inset with two glazed windows and a small gabled porch, which is slightly off set to the right-hand side of the building. It is clad entirely with a light-coloured grey stone and topped with matching slates. To my mind, John Neville must have come into money one way or another, as I just cannot believe that the poorer branch of the Neville family would be able to afford this type of building. As I survey the new wooden structure at the west end, I catch a glimpse of what I know to be flashing steel. Losing no time at all, I call out a warning.

Immediately, Alard and Ned run from the porch, each clutching an armful of rolls and parchments. Almost throwing them into the back of the cart, there is no time to waste. Morris pulls on the reins and both Ursula and I collapse onto our knees. Turning, we head for the main road and open ground, where ambush is almost impossible. My heart pounds as chaos breaks out. Finally, we are all together once more and travelling at speed in the direction of Sandal Castle and safety.

Arriving at Sandal Castle, the heavy wooden gates are swung wide open as we cross the moat and then promptly closed behind us. Collectively, we all breathe a sigh of relief. Stopping abruptly, just besides the walkway into the keep, Alard immediately jumps into the back of the cart and holds the sack open for Ursula to carefully place the rolls and parchments inside. Only time will tell if they hold the information that we seek. Unfortunately, due to my status as Lady Harsyck, I am unable to help in certain situations, for there are eyes everywhere and I must be prudent. I therefore sit alongside Morris at the front of the cart and survey the buildings within the inner bailey. They are extremely pleasant on the eye and clearly span a number of years. To my left is a small building, which I presume houses a well. Its roof is constructed from wood; it has five sloping sides and carved uprights. Behind is a finely timbered building, which has a wooden canopied walkway and in front of these stand a complex of exquisite stone buildings. They are built against the castle's outer wall and have glazed windows both at the upper and lower levels. How I long to climb the stone steps directly in front of us and explore within. At the end of the complex, there are many free-standing buildings. One has smoke billowing out from twin chimneys. I expect this to be an outside kitchen, something that is becoming increasingly fashionable nowadays. Then there is a bakery and some workshops.

Ursula and Alard, having finished packing the rolls and parchments, climb down from the cart before Davy reaches in and pulls the sack towards him. Alard, concerned for the safe-keeping of the documents, asks that they are taken to the library and placed under lock and key.

"Now, Ned, you know what needs to be done, and please remember that two clerks will begin translating the documents at first light, so you'll need to accompany them at all times."

As an afterthought, Alard adds, "Please keep the key safe."

Ned, intent on lighting the situation, immediately retorts, "What, do you think that I can't hold my ale and that I'll lose the key after supper?"

Unamused, Alard turns and waves his hand to summon two household retainers.

To my surprise, I recognise the retainers to be Peter of Pontefract and Simon of Sandal. Peter is the first to speak.

"Lady Harsyck, please let me help you down."

With this, Peter offers his hand, which I gratefully accept. I am unusually sore from the journey and I find it hard to straighten my back. Ursula, sensing my discomfort, gently rearranges my cloak about my shoulders. As she moves around me, I can see a deep loyalty in her eyes and I am grateful. I smile and thank Ursula, who is now fully immersed in her role as my lady-in-waiting. Heading towards the back of the cart, Ursula begins to supervise the unloading of my belongings. Ned, smiling at such a transformation, allows Ursula to direct proceedings.

"Now, Ned, please take Lady Harsyck's chest to her room, and Davy, please take my belongings to my room. I'll unpack in a little while, but before I do, I want to make sure that Lady Harsyck is comfortably seated. Alard, please could you accompany us and lead the way?"

As we approach the door to the keep, I see another face that I recognise. With great joy, I step forward and take both of Brother Pendlebury's hands.

"Welcome, Lady Harsyck, please do come inside."

Sensing that a cloak of trusted souls had been put in place to protect me, I wanted to find out a little more.

"I did not know that you would be here, Brother."

Brother Pendlebury smiles. "Ah… did I forget to mention that this is my home and that I would be returning with Peter and Simon?" Knowing full well that he did not mention this, Brother Pendlebury blushes. "Well, now that we have all safely arrived, it's time for us to rest in the great hall where refreshments are to be served."

Smiling broadly, I follow his lead.

Arriving at the great hall, I feel completely unprepared for the sheer number of people within. With a sorrowful frown, Brother Pendlebury explains that many of the villagers are still too traumatised to leave the castle and return to their homes.

"Alas, no one was prepared for the battle. We were caught unawares." Shaking his head, as tears begin to stream down his face, Brother Pendlebury continues, "To attack us when we were observing the birth of Christ seems a violation of the very worst kind. We were tricked, all of us. We foolishly believed that a truce had been called. That conflict had been averted for the twelve days of Christmas – and by the time we realised the truth, it was too late. Duke Richard called a Council of War here in this very room, the day before the battle. They were all here – Duke Richard; Edmund, Earl of Rutland; Richard, Earl of Salisbury; Sir Thomas Neville; Sir David Hall; Sir John Mortimer; Sir Hugh Mortimer and many, many more. The discussions lasted well into the night. The general consensus was to wait for Edward, Earl of March, to arrive with reinforcements, but Duke Richard would not have it. He just could not sit by and see his tenants brutally attacked and murdered, and law and order breakdown, while he sat within the safety of these walls. True to his sense of honour and bravery, he called to be armoured and surrounded by those loyal to him. The castle gates were opened and, well… you know the rest."

Shaking from Brother Pendlebury's moving account, I let Simon of Sandal and Ursula guide me to a cushioned seat that has been prepared for me at the top table. Seated, with Ursula on my right-hand side, I survey the sea of traumatised faces before me. Within moments, I am joined by Brother Pendlebury, who takes his seat to the left of me. Finally, we are joined by Morris, Owain, Davy, Ned and Alard.

The silence of the hall is broken by Simon of Sandal, who is now standing tall upon the dais. "Please, one and all, may I have your full attention, for I have some very exciting and unexpected news!" Simon then holds up a small roll of parchment and waves it above his head for all to see. "This is a letter from our glorious and valiant new king, Edward IV." A ripple of excitement reverberates around the hall. "I will read it word for word, so silence, if you please." Coughing to clear his throat, Simon begins, "To my father's most loyal and noble tenants, I write to you now, as if I were still Edward, Earl of March, to thank you for supporting my father, my brother, my uncle, and my cousin, to name but a few. I thank you for fighting bravely and for collecting all those who were killed on that most terrible day. Words can never express my gratitude and sadness. Such loss of life. Such treachery. Such deception. My heart is made heavy by the loss. It is now my turn to be loyal and to support you. My father would not wish you to be caged within the castle. Fearful of the future. He fought for freedom, and you must fight for that, too. To this end, I will be arriving with my retinue tomorrow. My retinue will build their camp outside of the castle walls. No doubt, there is still a risk of individual traitors, but I am content that the Battles of Mortimer's Cross and Towton have quelled the majority of dissent. We will stay for a few days, and these will be spent rebuilding your homes and securing your fields. Once the fencing has been repaired, I will send word to

Pontefract, so that the drovers will bring piglets, calves and lambs to restock your farms. You will then be able to return to the normality of daily life, and we will leave you and travel onwards to London, where we will enter the city in triumph. However, before we leave, we will all celebrate the feast of Easter together." Again, ripples of shock reverberate around the hall. Simon speaks once more, "As you see, we have much to do in preparation. Tonight, we will eat heartily and drink to King Edward – for tomorrow, the work begins."

I awake to the most glorious of days. The sun is streaming in through a montage of small green glazed glass panels and proceeds to dance upon the floor. I can hear Ursula singing sweetly in the attached solar, as she lays out my clothing for the day ahead. In the background, I can also hear birdsong and activity within the inner bailey. Remembering King Edward's letter and the great excitement in the hall after Simon read it aloud, I smile broadly for the first time in weeks. It feels so good to have something to look forward to. Easter with King Edward and his household… what could be better?

Ursula calls from within the solar. "Mistress Bethany, your clothes are ready. May I come in and prepare your hair?"

"Yes, of course, Ursula. My comb is in my satchel. You are very welcome to go inside and get it." After a shaky start, I really rather like having help. Throwing back the linen sheet and coverlet, I immediately feel the gentle warmth of the spring sunshine on my body.

A very excited Ursula comes rushing in. "Oh, Mistress Bethany, how exciting – King Edward is coming here! There is so much to do. I was downstairs in the kitchen earlier, where everything is buzzing. The hall is having a thorough spring-clean, and maids are carrying as much linen as they can hold down to the river to be washed and dried in readiness. Alard, Owain and Ned are hard at work cleaning the best pewter and silver tableware, while Davy is stuffing dried herbs into linen bags and Morris is directing operations in the stables." Ursula stops to chuckle. "When I last saw Morris, he was completely covered in straw." Without drawing breath, she continues, "I have been put in charge of preparing King Edward's bedchamber. His bedding and cushions are arriving this afternoon. Oh, I am so excited. Have you ever seen a more handsome man."

I smile and contemplate Ursula's comment. Yes, King Edward is handsome in the extreme. His hair is like spun gold and his smile is like pure sunshine, but I'd say that my Pip is the most handsome man ever. I picture his rugged beauty, his kind eyes, his soft mouth and his gentle ways. Loyal and dependable. How I miss Pip. Perhaps our paths might cross again; maybe on the way to Fotheringhay Castle. In my mind, I make a mental note to speak to Alard about joining King Edward's baggage train. The protection that it would afford us would be most welcome, but I'm sure that Alard has everything perfectly under control.

Realising that Ursula is still waiting for a reply, I decide not to mention the possibility of travelling with King Edward's baggage train, as I would hate to build up her hopes and then dash them. "Yes, Ursula, King Edward is a most fine man – a true 'Sun in Splendour.'"

Secretly sharing Ursula's excitement, I stand and happily gaze out of the solar window. Just beyond the castle walls, King Edward's encampment is being prepared. Trenches are being dug, and barrels of water are being put in place around the outer edges of the field. Later, tents and canopies will be erected. I can also make out the fire pits and ironwork for cooking. As is always the case, not all household members enjoy the communal living of the hall. Some like to cook for themselves.

Speaking of kitchens, I remember Alard's invitation to join everyone. "Ursula, are you ready to join the others?"

"Oh yes, Mistress, I'm so excited to explore the castle."

"Well, let's go then."

Leaving the solar, I resume my persona of Lady Harsyck. Ursula, having already acquainted herself with the route to and from the kitchen, proceeds at a pace and we make swift progress. The castle appears to be a maze of long passageways with a great many rooms leading off them. All of the passageways are plastered and painted a deep burnt orange. Whatever dye was used, it has been mixed perfectly, as I cannot see a single flaw or imperfection. Heavy drapes and embroideries further adorn the walls.

As we pass the chapel, I stop to gaze inside. Its simplicity is beautiful. The first thing that catches my eye is a finely carved wooden stand, which is topped with an earth-coloured jug and matching bowl. Alongside, there is a pile of linen squares. Steam emanates from the jug and I can smell rose petals. I suspect that hot water is always readily available and that it is topped up as soon as footsteps are heard entering the passageway. My eye is then drawn to a finely glazed window at the furthest end of the chapel. It is made up of mainly plain glass with just three emblems. The Mortimer shield, a white rose and a falcon sitting within a fetterlock, which is slightly ajar. Reading it from left to right, it tells the story of Duke Richard. His family, his very being and his patience. Ready to swoop into action at a moment's notice, the falcon is merely resting.

Then, below the window, I catch my first glimpse of Duke Richard's moveable altar from the Holy Land that Brother Pendlebury spoke of. Entering the chapel, closely followed by Ursula, we kneel before it. The stone altar is box-shaped and has carvings of saints all around it. Then, there are niches of varying depths. It has four sturdy feet and it must be at least three hands high. At its base, set within the largest niche, is a collection of incredibly small unbleached linen packages, all of which appear extremely ancient. They sit within a shallow glass bowl. Each is bound with a cord and they all have handwritten italic linen tags. I can just about decipher the Latin inscriptions and, to my amazement, the tags appear to indicate that within are the relics of St Francis of Assisi. I cross myself and seek to enrich myself with the healing powers that no doubt radiate from them. Sensing Ursula's longing to leave, I stand, bow low and indicate for Ursula to do the same.

The noise emanating from the kitchen is almost deafening. I can hear orders being given, laughing and, yes, even Ned's shawm somewhere in the distance! I smile within, as I imagine Alard's irritation at the noise. Ursula, keen to look after me, smooths my cloak and straightens my coif before entering. To our delight, there is a table laden with food.

After a flurry of good mornings, we head directly towards the assortment of breads. Owain, who is helping the cook, stops what he's doing and comes over to serve us.

"Thank you, Owain, but please don't let us interrupt you. We can just as easily serve ourselves."

Owain nods gratefully and announces that he is compiling a list of provisions for King Edward's visit and that Cook Rouen is compiling a list of dishes to serve the king. Scratching his head, Owain looks concerned. "Let's hope that the household's fishing skills are up to scratch, as we'll need a great deal of fish over the next couple of days."

At this, Cook Rouen looks up and smiles. "There's no need to worry about that, lad. We're used to catering for very large numbers at little notice. We have a full stock of salt fish and plenty of vegetables laid down in the ice-pits. Then, there's the new crop of nettles and wild garlic to freshen up the old leeks and greens. I also still have masses of onions, turnips and apples in store. You never know, Father Paul may even grant special permission for me to serve some restricted Lenten foods – but even if he doesn't, I can make the finest almond milk pottage with dried apple, onion tarts, green peas and fried beans. What's more, I could also cook King Edward's favourite – spiced apple fritters in an ale batter. I've known the king ever since he was a child, as I used to cook for him and his brother, Edmund, Earl of Rutland, at Ludlow Castle whenever Duke Richard was in residence." With this, Cook Rouen crosses himself.

Within a few moments, the situation is lightened again, as we are joined by a very buoyant Ned. "Lady Harsyck, will you join me in the library once you have broken your fast? Then we can supervise the two clerks and the translation of the documents together."

Overjoyed to be invited to join in, I gratefully accept Ned's invitation. Alard, on the other hand, is not so joyous. "Ned, didn't I tell you to supervise the clerks at all times."

"Yes, that you did and that's what I've been doing. The

clerks have stopped for a short break, so I decided to hunt down some refreshments."

Alard, appearing appeased, smiles and announces that there is more than enough food for everyone to break their fasts.

Once sated, I leave Ursula to explore the castle with Owain, while I return to the library with Ned. Somehow, I have never thought of Ned as a man of letters, but it would seem that I am wrong. For once, we have been joined by the two clerks and the library door is locked firmly behind us. Ned carefully removes each roll, one at a time, before removing any cords or ribbons. Then, he gently unrolls the parchment and examines it for any water damage or inserted sections, before scanning for any names or places. Once satisfied that the documents are true and that they have no obvious signs of tampering, Ned divides them into two piles. Looking up, Ned explains that unsealed documents can be fraudulent, as water damage can be a sign that the documents have had their words either removed or changed, and that false sections are often used as a means of changing timelines.

"Ned, I am curious – why two piles?"

Pointing to the left-hand pile, Ned explains, "Those ones appear uninteresting, but they need to be read and documented anyway. Whereas the ones over there have sentences in them that concern me. I would bet my purse of pennies that they hold hidden meanings."

"What sort of hidden messages?"

"I'm not really sure, but the way that they are constructed doesn't quite ring true. I know that everyone uses language differently, but even the differences are consistent and the words spelt correctly, whereas, if you look here, this sentence looks like secret codes."

At first, I can't see anything, but then I notice that some of the words have numbers instead of letters. "Have you come across this before Ned?"

"Yes, occasionally. People often insert numbers instead of letters or they write the occasional letter back to front. The first thing is to identify the pattern of numbers and letters and then to write all the words down, one after the other. Sometimes a code will appear immediately, whereas at other times it takes much longer to decipher, and it's not just the words that need to be checked. Sometimes dots and dashes are placed around the parchment in seemingly random places, but at other times they can be placed in specific places. Look, I'll show you." Ned then picks up a quill, dips it in the ink and places three very faint dots at the top of the page. "Now, these could be taken as three irregular splashes of ink, or they could mean 'meet at three o'clock in the north', and if you add the letter L, that could mean 'meet at three o'clock, at the north entrance of Ludlow' or maybe London."

Amazed at such attention to detail, I do not envy either the clerks or Ned. Deciding that my presence would be a distraction, I excuse myself from the library and leave Ned and the clerks to complete their fascinating work. Once more alone, I make my way up to the battlements. Climbing the last section is quite challenging, as each of the steps are of different proportions. To my surprise, when I eventually look up, I see Peter of Pontefract with an outstretched arm.

"Lady Harsyck, this is an unexpected pleasure. What brings you here?"

I gladly take Peter's hand as the final step is much higher than the others. "Well, it's a bit hard to explain really, but, basically, I feel the need to see the battlefield."

Peter's eyes display a deep sadness and I can see that he completely understands, as he turns to lead the way. The battlements are very narrow, far more so than I had imagined. As I walk, I have to keep smoothing my cloak down to stop it becoming caught on the rough stones.

"Now, Lady Harsyck, please be incredibly careful along this section, as the turrets here are incredibly low. Before the battle, the stonemasons were replacing some of the very old stones."

To steady myself, I press the right-hand side of my body closer to the wall. The stones are cold, but somehow comforting. Running my hand over them, I immediately feel indentations. On closer inspection, I see a sign. It is inlaid with flint and shaped like a star. "Peter, please could you tell me about this?"

"Yes, of course. There are symbols all along the wall. They tell the archers all the information that they need to know. Where the sun rises, where the sun sets, and where is best to defend from."

"Really? How can they know that?"

"Well, each of the fields are numbered and let's say that the castle is being attacked from field one; the bell in the courtyard chimes once and then all the archers know where they are needed."

"That is so clever – is that the same in every castle?"

"Oh no. To my understanding, it's only Duke Richard's castles that use the system. He was always trialling new methods, and he loved building."

Pride instantly wells up within me. However, this feeling doesn't last too long and is soon overtaken by a deep trauma as Peter stops and points to the battlefield. Right in front of me, I can see the deeply churned earth, where the soil has been scarred by death. Reeling from the knowledge that this is where Richard, Duke of York was killed, my head begins to spin around and around. The dizziness is all encompassing. Then, I begin to feel acid rising from my stomach into my throat. I clasp my chest to help me breath. In the distance, I can just about make out Wakefield Bridge and the Chantry Chapel of St Mary the Virgin, where John Clifford cruelly murdered Earl Edmund. Silently, I fall to the ground. Wedged in between two walls and laying on my back, all I can see now is a sky laden with dark clouds. My anger erupts and I scream out loud. How could Clifford have murdered him in cold blood? Poor Edmund; how awful to have been trapped within sight of sanctuary. I torment myself by imagining Clifford's sword being held aloft. How I detest that man. A butcher of the vilest order. I am glad that he was cut down the day before the Battle of Towton, and that he now lies dead. I hope that he rots in Hell for what he did and I'm going to make sure that all traitors get their comeuppance.

Taking Peter's hand, I rise from the floor. My anger is such that I feel no embarrassment. Then, all of a sudden, I notice the deep wound that lies beneath Peter's sleeve. It looks relatively new. "Thank you, Peter. Your arm. Please tell me where you got that wound?"

Peter shifts from one foot to another as tears begin to stream down his face. "I got that as I threw myself on top of the earl, as they knocked him to the ground. I tried to give my life, to save his, but I was attacked by a group of Clifford's men. I was helplessly outnumbered. They kicked me to one side and held me down. I just couldn't move. God help me, I saw the fatal blow and could do nothing. I wish that they had killed me, too, but instead they just laughed and left me to live with my shame."

"Peter, you should bear no shame. You tried your hardest. Would you know those men again if you saw them?"

"Oh yes, their faces are imprinted into my brain. Each time I try to sleep, I can see their faces and hear their taunts. I can also see Edmund's lifeless body. His blood pooling on the ground. I will say no more, though, as I wish to spare you from such evil."

Grateful for Peter's consideration, and not wishing to be sick, I hold his hands to stop them from shaking. "Peter, will you accompany me on my journey to track down the traitors?"

Without hesitation, Peter agrees and we retrace our steps along the battlements, across the courtyard and into the kitchen.

As I enter, I can see Morris sitting, covered in dust, in front of the fire. He is eating a huge chunk of pie. There are crumbs everywhere and he has a look of contentment on his face. I attempt to block out all thoughts of death from my mind and instead I try to concentrate on the king's impending visit.

Seeing me enter, Morris stands immediately. "Good day, Lady Harsyck."

Laughing at Morris's appearance, I bid that he sits once more and continues. "You look like you're enjoying that pie, Morris."

"Oh yes, it's grand. Would you like me to fetch you a slice?"

"No, thank you, I ate rather too much bread this morning and I'm still full." Taking a seat, I happily listen to the last-minute plans.

Alard, double-checking that everything is in order, mumbles loudly as he goes through each item. “Well, that’s everything in hand, for now, and as soon as Davy and Owain have supervised the storing of the fish in the ice-pit, it would seem that we are finished.”

I look around the kitchen for Ursula, but she is missing. Concerned for her welfare, I ask Alard as to her whereabouts.

With a huge smile, Alard replies that she is still supervising the king’s bedchamber. “I have heard from the other ladies that she is rearranging the king’s bedchamber for the fourth time, but I’m not entirely convinced that the king will really mind how it’s laid out nor how the cushions have been plumped.”

We all chuckle and are glad to enjoy the lightness of the moment.

After what seems an age, Ursula and four pretty housemaids enter the kitchen. Each of them looking tired but content. The eldest immediately heads towards the watered ale and pours a mug for each of them, before taking a large swig.

“Oh, how I needed that. Come on, girls, let’s get a drink inside of you.”

Stunned by her outgoing nature, I am surprised when she goes red upon seeing me.

“Lady Harsyck, please accept my apologies. I did not see you there. I should not have spoken in such a way in your presence. Please forgive me.”

Standing, I smile and say that she has nothing to apologise for. “Has Ursula been working you to a frazzle?”

“Yes, she’s a hard taskmaster, but the room looks grand.”

Noting that Ursula is a little embarrassed, I nod towards the door when no one is looking and, from the look on Ursula’s face, I note that she wishes to leave. "I hope that you will all enjoy your rest. Alas, I must take Ursula with me as there is some sewing that we must finish before the king's visit."

After a flurry of curtsies, we leave and make our way to the solar. Once inside, Ursula flops onto the cushioned window seat.

"Thank you so much, Mistress. I am exhausted, but I didn't want to offend anyone by leaving. Most of the housemaids are very nice, but I don't like Millie – the very loud one. She has said that she plans on making herself available to the king, if you know what I mean. She plans on getting pregnant with his illegitimate child and never working again. I am so worried that if I tell any of the men, they may make it obvious, and I am fearful of her tongue."

"Don't worry about that, Ursula. Now that you have told me, I can think up a way of removing all the housemaids and, indeed, all the temptation from the king."

Smiling, we sit in silence and rest. After spending a great deal of time in the king's company, I am reminded that he really does need as much temptation removed as possible.

Now rested, Ursula and I sit side by side on the window seat and scour the horizon for movement. As the light begins to fade, we spot the king and his retinue advancing at a steady pace. His Standard fluttering in the evening breeze. The king is on his way!

Ursula rises immediately and quickly helps me to change into my new dark-green woollen kirtle. This evening, I will still wear my brown coif and brown cloak for mourning purposes, but I wish to reflect a little of my joy. Once ready, we sit and wait in the solar for Owain to collect us. I decide that now is as good a time as any to show Ursula just how grateful I am for her support. So, I fumble in my satchel and pull out a small package that I had Owain prepare for me yesterday. Wrapped in pale-blue silk, I can feel its weight and shape. Turning to face Ursula, I note just how tired she looks.

"Ursula, before Owain comes, I have something to give you. A thank you for everything that you do for me."

Ursula, with a look of surprise, takes the gift and examines it from all angles. "Thank you, Mistress, but I don't know what to say. No one's ever given me a surprise present before."

"Well, they have now."

With trembling hands, Ursula unfolds the silk. Taking her time, I can see that she is cherishing each moment. On opening it, Ursula's face lights up immediately. "Oh, it's beautiful… thank you so much! You really shouldn't have! It's just so beautiful!"

Taking the necklace from Ursula's shaking hands, I secure it firmly about her neck. The silver glints in the soft evening candlelight and the enamelled sun pendant falls perfectly into place. Clasping the pendant, Ursula proclaims that she will wear it forever before hugging me tightly.

We can hear Owain's footsteps long before he knocks on the door. Having both regained our composure, Ursula opens the door.

A grinning Owain refrains from mentioning the pendant and instead asks, "Lady Harsyck, are you ready to join the king's welcoming party?"

Nodding, I smile and try to control my excitement. "Yes, Owain, please lead the way."

To my surprise, we turn the opposite way to normal and descend a small winding staircase, which brings us out by the main gatehouse. Joined by Alard, Davy, Ned and Morris, we stand directly in front of the other members of the household. With Simon of Sandal and Peter of Pontefract taking up their places either side of the large wooden gate, Brother Pendlebury stands patiently to receive the king. Outside, I can hear the sound of horses hooves coming to an abrupt halt. Men are shouting, "Hurrah!" at the top of their voices and the gate swings open. Then, the music begins. Ned, intent on welcoming the king in the loudest possible manner, blows with energy into his shawm. Walking forward, Brother Pendlebury bows low before King Edward and then straightens slowly.

"Welcome and praise the Lord that you are here. Glorious King Edward, I thank you wholeheartedly for bringing hope to us all."

The king then smiles and leans forward to whisper into Brother Pendlebury's ear, before cheekily announcing that the journey has left him with a dry mouth, and that he is sure that the others will be equally afflicted, so perhaps a tankard of ale for all would be the order of the day. Alard, taking over from Brother Pendlebury, introduces everyone. In truth, very few are unknown to the king, but to keep up appearances, and to preserve my disguise, neither of us show any signs of having met before.

Inside, Davy quickly enacts my plan of action to keep Millie and the other housemaids occupied and out of sight. They are instructed to pour the refreshments and then to await further instructions from inside the kitchen. Delighted that my plan has worked seamlessly, I happily follow everyone into the great hall, take my seat and wait for the evening's festivities to begin. Surveying the hall, I can see relieved faces all around and I can feel a tangible sense of calm in the air. In essence, the king's visit has worked, even before it has truly begun. Normality has been restored. There is no doubt about it, people now have renewed hope and they long to return to their homes in the morning.

Once refreshed, the food is served to the rhythm of a drum. Ned, having changed his tack, is now standing at the back of the hall with a tabor suspended from his neck. It's not the largest drum that I have ever seen, but it may well be the loudest that I have ever heard. The body of the drum is circular and is roughly two hands across. It's made of wood, cord and animal skin. Ned, not content with just striking the drum, is now juggling the drumsticks. Throwing them high in the air, he spins on the spot before catching them. For once, Alard is laughing wholeheartedly.

The food is delicious. I have never eaten almond milk pottage with dried apples before. It is creamy, thick and has a tangy sweetness about it. Tonight, there are three removes, but I decide to leave the second, as salt fish has never been a favourite of mine. I sit and wait in anticipation of the spiced apple fritters and contemplate the ale batter. Luckily, I do not have to wait too long. When it is served, it exceeds all of my expectations. Still steaming hot, butter oozes from the fritters. The batter is very crispy and a golden-brown colour. I can see why it would be one of King Edward's favourite dishes. Unable to control myself, I take another portion when it is offered to me.

Once finished, I look across at Ursula, who sits at the head of the side table, positioned between Morris and Davy. I can see that despite her tiredness, she is enjoying herself. She is smiling and laughing, and every so often, she clasps the sun pendant in her delicate little hand. I am glad that she is happy.

I then sit forward very slightly to see King Edward's face. I can see sadness in his eyes and, on closer inspection, I can see tear stains on his cheeks. It must be horrendously difficult to put on a brave face when everywhere reminds you of what you have lost. However, in true fighting spirit, he raises his hand and beckons Ned over. Ned, immediately at the king's side, falls to his knees. I suspect that there is mischief afoot as both of them are now grinning from ear to ear. Upon rising, Ned beckons for Alard, Morris and Davy to join them. After huddling together for a few minutes, Ned leaves the hall.

In his absence, Alard, Morris and Davy go from soul to soul, clearing tables and pushing them back against the walls. Youngsters are invited to sit cross-legged in front of their elders, and a large space in the middle of the hall is cleared. King Edward begins to clap in a slow rhythmic fashion. Bringing his hands together firmly, he stands on the dais and invites everyone to join in with him. Before long, the atmosphere is electric. With a loud bang, a hidden door opens and Ned enters. Dressed only in knee-length breeches, he bounds in. Laughter fills the air. Ned's pale white body flexes as he begins to sway from side to side. Then, King Edward begins to clap once more, but this time he claps quickly and in a manic fashion. Ned disappears momentarily, before returning with two pairs of flaming drumsticks, which he then proceeds to juggle. People gasp with both fear and delight as his bare feet slap on the floor in perfect timing to King Edward's clapping. Then, with a final flourish, Ned extinguishes each drumstick with a huge breath of air, before running towards the dais and bowing low before the king. In keeping with the jest, King Edward proceeds to knight Ned and pronounces him 'King of the Night'. Loud clapping and cheering fills the air. Ned, turning to face the hall, bids that everyone despatch the night as they see fit, before blowing kisses to one and all, and disappearing through the once-concealed doorway.

Make Haste to Conisbrough

On waking, I remember that today is Maundy Thursday and, for once, I am alone. Today, I will prepare myself for the day ahead, as Ursula, having woken especially early, is in attendance upon the king in his chambers. I am immensely proud that Ursula has been asked to join King Edward's close confidants this morning, as I will not always require a lady-in-waiting and, this way, it will not seem strange if and when she joins the king's household for good.

Shortly, I am to join Ned and the clerks. I hear from Owain that Ned's work is almost complete and I am excited to find out more. However, before I rise, I lay for a little while longer and listen to the sounds from outside. I can hear all sorts of commotion. In the distance, there are loud thuds, which I presume are related to the fencing work. Closer to home, I can hear a cart trundle around the inner bailey and a rather loud voice issuing instructions. Intrigued, I rise and make my way to the window. Pulling my cloak about myself, I lean forward to see a rather short fat man standing below. He appears to be directing operations and, if I'm not mistaken, it is our cart that is being loaded. It looks like a quick exit is being planned, as Morris is standing to one side and waving his hands frantically around. With my curiosity now aroused, I dress quickly. Today, I will wear my brown woollen kirtle and matching cloak, a plain white coif and my very old leather boots, which are extremely comfortable.

Leaving the room, I turn and lock the door, before attaching the large iron key to my girdle. The passageways are unusually empty and I make my way with speed to the library. How strange – the door is wide open and I can see no movement within. Investigating further, I enter and look around. All of the desks are empty and there are no rolls of parchment or baskets anywhere to be seen. Startled by a noise behind me, I immediately turn around to see a heavily shrouded figure standing in the doorway. Fear courses through my body, but I refuse to move.

"Who are you and what do you want?" The figure refuses to speak. So, I ask once more with an edge to my voice, "Who are you and what do you want in this place?"

This time, the figure steps forward and, with one purposeful push, slams the door closed. Trapped and realising that there is no point in screaming, I stand stock still and ask again. "What do you mean by your actions?"

With this, the figure moves even closer. So much so that I can feel a man's breath upon my face. Deciding that my only course of action is to escape, I attempt to push past the figure and open the door. I frantically pull on the door handle until I release that it is no good – the latch is jammed solid from the force of being slammed shut. The figure now grasps my wrist with a gloved hand and pulls me back. Confused at such an ambush in a supposedly safe place, I am forced to change my plan. If I can't escape or call for help, I have no option but to deal with the situation.

Turning to face the figure, I begin, "Well, if you won't speak to me, perhaps you would be kind enough to show yourself to me or, at least, tell me your name?"

With this, the man's body rises and falls as if laughing at me.

"I'm glad that you're amused, as I most certainly am not." Anger wells up inside me. I attempt to release his hand from my wrist, but the more I struggle the tighter his grip becomes. Now he pulls me even closer. So close that I can smell mint upon his breath. Deciding that if I am to be attacked, I need to see his face for future identification, I grab his hood with my free hand and try to pull it down, but I am too slow. Within seconds, his lips are upon mine and his arms around me. Locked in his embrace, I feel my fear vanish immediately, for I would know those tender lips anywhere. On opening my eyes, I see Pip gazing at me with such love.

"My darling Bethany, please forgive me. I desperately needed to see you and to make sure that you were safe. I came in disguise, as I cannot afford to be seen, and then I had the stupid idea of seeing how you would deal with a dangerous, maybe deadly, situation. Oh, my darling, I can see now that I need not have ever worried, as you are a fierce and brave combatant, and one who is not easily defeated. In future, though, please never go anywhere alone. I will send word to Alard and make plans for your future safety. Sandal is on the whole safe, but beyond these walls there is danger everywhere."

Pip's voice fades and his face is etched with worry. He continues, "Darling, we have only been apart for a few days, but in those days my heart feels broken. I fear for you constantly and I dread leaving you alone to track down the traitors. However, I know that if I accompany you, suspicions will be aroused. I'm so sorry that I tested you." Pip kisses me once more.

Overjoyed at being in Pip's arms, I feel no annoyance, only love. "Well, you gave me quite a shock and, to be completely honest, I was absolutely terrified. I thought that I was going to be raped or murdered, or both. I tried to be strong, but I agree, I will never ever walk anywhere ever again on my own."

Relief floods over us both, before we kiss once more. Then, to my surprise, Pip takes a step backwards.

"I'm so sorry, my darling, but I fear that the time has come for me to leave you. Ned will be back soon with the clerks. He has identified a lead. It would appear that Richard Neville, Earl of Warwick may be one of the traitors and, as such, you must leave here today and begin your travels across country to Warwick Castle. If the rumours are true, then King Edward, along with his brothers, are all in danger, for any man that can betray his own father, uncle and brother can betray anyone. Time is of the essence."

With those words, I begin to shake. I cling onto Pip and kiss him once more, dreading the moment that he has to leave. Tears flood down my face. In the distance, Ned's voice can be heard. Pip, looking startled, draws up his hood and stands to the side of the door. I, on the other hand, stand directly in front of it. Outside, Ned is now throwing his full weight against the door and grumbling that it will not open. Eventually, the latch loosens itself and the door swings open at an alarming speed. In the confusion of the moment, Ned –

accompanied by two clerks – enters, as Pip stealthily leaves. Noticing my tears, Ned looks concerned.

"Bethany, you poor thing. How long have you been in here? Did the door lock on you? Did someone lock you in?"

Knowing that the clerks are listening to each word, I decide to say nothing of Pip's visit, for they may be enemy informants. Choking back the tears, I eventually speak, "I came to see you, as I thought that we could break our fast together and somehow the door slammed shut and I just couldn't open it." Feeling myself blush at such a lie, I look down at the floor.

"Well, no harm done, and breaking our fast sounds like an excellent idea to me."

Before we leave, Ned thanks the clerks for their diligence and bids them a fond farewell. Descending the spiral staircase, Ned stops and looks at me. Smiling, he asks, "Bethany, I don't suppose that you've had a secret visitor, have you?" Unable to keep a secret from Ned, I nod and smile enthusiastically. "I thought so. I thought that I could smell mint in the air."

In the kitchen, we find Alard, Owain and Davy huddled around the fireplace deep in conversation, while Morris sits with the short fat man at the centre table. I decide to join Morris, while Ned joins the men. As I approach, they both stand. The short fat man appears a little startled by my presence. Bowing low, he welcomes me as Lady Harsyck.

"Good day, Lady Harsyck, I am very pleased to meet you. Please let me introduce myself; my name is Baldwin and I am Morris's nephew."

Looking at one and then the other, I can see a family similarity. For although they appear completely different in most respects, they have exactly the same shaped nose.

Long and wide with a wart at the tip. Morris, noticing my scrutiny, proudly announces that Baldwin is his sister Lizzy's son.

"Ah yes, Baldwin belongs to our Lizzy alright. She's a daft soul, like myself, but she's given life to two strong lads. Baldwin and his younger brother, Bertram. Both fine specimens and completely loyal to the House of York. She chose their names with great care. 'Baldwin' meaning 'brave friend' and 'Bertrum' meaning 'bright raven'." Morris chuckles and then shakes his head before announcing, "Daft Lizzy."

To my surprise, Cook Rouen appears from seemingly nowhere with an extremely large sack of flour thrown over his left shoulder. "Good morrow, Lady Harsyck, I hope that you are well and rested after the events of last night."

I smile. "Oh yes, last night was such fun and I loved every mouthful of the feast. I can see why the spiced apple fritters with ale batter are one of King Edward's favourite dishes. They were absolutely delicious."

"Well, if you thought that they were delicious, I can't wait to hear what you think about the fritters that I'm just about to prepare for tonight's feast."

Overhearing my conversation with Cook Rouen, Alard comes over and sits down next to me. "I'm really sorry, Mistress, but we must leave immediately. I have sent word to Ursula and have asked her to pack up all your belongings as quickly as possible."

Remembering the key at my waist, I free it from my girdle and hand it over to Alard. "Ah, Ursula may have problems, as here is the key to my room."

"Oh, that's not a problem at all, as the Steward of Sandal holds a complete set of master keys."

Leaving the warmth of the kitchen, I shudder at the icy cold air. Looking up, I notice that the sky is laden with heavy snow clouds. I pray that the snow holds off. Climbing aboard the cart, I sit once again next to Morris.

"Here we go again, Mistress. Now settle yourself and make sure that you wrap that sheepskin tightly around your back and legs. We've not got far to travel, but, as you can see, snow threatens and an icy wind blows. Davy and Owain have gone to collect your trunk, Ned is securing the rolls, and Alard is accompanying Ursula." Turning to face me, Morris appears concerned. "Mistress Bethany, I have something that I must tell you. Ursula will not be travelling with us anymore. We are to leave her here, at Sandal. Alard says that it's for the best and I agree wholeheartedly." Attempting to lighten the mood, Morris continues, "So, it's just the six of us again, along with Liege, Freemantle and Peter of Pontefract thrown in for good measure."

Morris's news does not surprise me, as I had expected Ursula to join the king's household at some point. I just didn't know when. Ursula now comes into view and, upon seeing me, runs towards the cart with outstretched arms. Tears are streaming down her face, and her eyes are red and swollen.

"Oh, Mistress. I wish that I could stay with you forever and remain your lady-in-waiting. I know that it's only been a few days, but I long to serve you and be by your side. I know that I will miss you with all of my heart, but Alard says that I must stay here." With these words, the mood changes and Ursula glares at Alard with a look of pure hatred.

Confused, I ask, "Are you to join the king's household?"

"No. I am to stay here before returning to my village, where I will be married."

Shocked at the news, I sit back and consider what I have just heard. "Return to your village and marry? You never mentioned that you were betrothed."

"I am not."

Morris, taking up the reins, shakes them gently in a bid to get away. "Well, that's enough of that, Ursula. You must do as you are told and that's an end to it. Don't go upsetting Lady Harsyck."

Shockingly, as we pull away, Ursula attempts to throw herself to the ground in front of Liege. Stopping abruptly, Morris becomes angry.

"Don't you go scaring my horses. You'll pay for it if you do. Now, go away!" Hearing this, Simon of Sandal appears from the gatehouse and drags Ursula to one side. "She's a mad one, she is, and I'll be glad to see the back of her."

"But Morris, why? Ursula appears to be hard-working, honest and true."

"Well, that's as it may be, but she's let herself down good and proper this morning. She was supposed to be helping the king get ready for the day ahead, and instead she climbed into his bed and tempted him when no one was looking. Somehow, by the grace of God, King Edward was restrained for once and, apparently, he just laughed, before having her removed."

Shocked at such antics, I now wonder if Ursula's story about Millie making herself available to the king was just a lie and whether it was actually Ursula all along who planned to conceive the king's illegitimate child. Either way, Ursula is now writhing on the floor and clawing at her own throat in the manner of a madwoman. Not knowing what to do, I sit in silence and watch.

"Take that, Mistress, for I have no further need of it. It is clear from your silence that you will not save me and I want nothing of yours to remind me of this place."

To my horror, the enamelled sun pendant, which I gave to Ursula last night, now lies broken and in pieces on the ground.

In what seems like no time at all, the great cylindrical keep of Conisbrough Castle comes into view. I have heard of this place many times before. Not only was it the home of Richard, Earl of Cambridge and his beautiful wife, Anne Mortimer. It was the birthplace of Richard, Duke of York and home to my distant ancestors. I am so excited to enter and explore. I have no idea of how long we will stay, but I'm determined to make the most of every moment. I have left the upset and disappointment of Ursula's actions behind me. In fact, the events of the last few hours have taught me that I don't really need a lady-in-waiting at all, but I do need a protector and Peter of Pontefract fits the bill perfectly. What good would Ursula have been if the figure in the library had been a malevolent one?

As we meet the rising ground, the snow begins to steadily fall. It clings to our cloaks and covers everything in its wake. Liege and Freemantle shake their heads and gently jig around, making their discomfort known.

Morris, looking towards the sky, announces his concerns. "Ah well, we've made it in good time, Mistress. I was fearful of the snow arriving earlier, but we had no choice. We had to leave when we did. We needed to get the rolls to safety and the keep of Conisbrough Castle is ten times as secure as anywhere else. Yorkist to its core, Conisbrough Castle is the safest place to be." Patting Morris's hand, I smile and feel a deep sense of relief at having arrived. "We'll be inside before you know it, Mistress."

On hearing these words, Davy mumbles aloud, "Praise the Lord. I'm freezing and my feet are wet."

Ned, as mischievous as ever, calls out, "Davy, you are always moaning."

To this, Owain and Peter laugh. Alard, however, is not so cruel; he just lowers his head and smiles.

Passing over the deep moat and trundling through a succession of gates, Morris goes on, "Forgive me if I speak out of turn, Mistress, but I'm glad that Ursula was left behind. I did not like sharing your company."

Smiling, I can see that Morris is right. "Morris, I, too, am glad that we left Ursula behind. It was extremely tiring having to be guarded all the time. I can now focus all of my energies on the journey and the task in hand."

As we enter the inner bailey, we are met by a group of about twenty retainers, who are all dressed in pale blue and white livery. Immediately, I feel safe and sound. Choosing to remain in the cart, I await instructions before climbing down. Watching on, I note how Owain and Ned pass the rolls to the retainers for safe-keeping and storage. For it is imperative that they are taken inside immediately. All the while, Morris and Davy seek to free Liege and Freemantle from their reins, while Alard instructs the retainers to remove the remaining luggage from the cart.

"Come along, Mistress Bethany, let me get you inside. You'll catch your death of cold out here." With those words, Peter reaches up and lifts me down from the cart. "I can't have you slipping now, can I?"

Inside, the air is warm and moist, and there is a strong smell of dried lavender, which has been infused with rose oil. We are welcomed by a tall, thin elderly man. He is wearing a long dark-green velvet robe lined with ermine. His robe is gathered at the waist by a thin green leather belt and he has matching green leather shoes.

"Lady Harsyck, it is such an honour to meet you. I am aware of your lineage and your very special links to Conisbrough and our dear-departed Countess of Cambridge. I remember the countess with such fondness, for I was just a boy when she passed away. My name is Osbert de Mortimer, one of the stewards of Conisbrough Castle." He bows, before leading me to a rather fine but worn padded chair that resembles a throne. "My role is to look after the castle and to make sure that all of the legal matters associated with the castle and the manor are handled in a timely and correct fashion."

Feeling relaxed, safe and warm, I sink into the cushioned chair and thank Osbert for his hospitality. Intrigued, I ask, "You say *one* of the stewards – does Conisbrough have more than one?"

Nodding, Osbert responds, "Yes, there are two of us. I look after the legal matters, while Robert Boydell, who you will meet later, looks after the household in its entirety. I believe that, as we speak, Robert is overseeing the preparation of the Holy Thursday meal, which will be served after Father John de Bocking has finished washing the altar with water and wine, and has blessed the oils, in readiness for the year ahead. Perhaps you would like to rest for a short while upstairs in your chamber. I know that it has been prepared for you and that it is ready."

After careful consideration, I decide to stay put. "That's very kind of you, but I'm happy here and I long to spend time with the others."

Osbert nods and smiles before leaving.

Sitting by the huge stone fireplace in the lower-level chamber of the solar, I allow myself to daydream about my encounter with Pip. Oh, how I wish that he were here now. I wonder where he is and I pray that he is safe. However, the silence does not last too long as the others soon join me. Flushed from the sudden warmth of the room, they take their seats and immediately remove their boots. Davy appears to be in pain and is rubbing his foot vigorously.

"Are you alright, Davy? What's wrong? Are you hurt?"

"That bloody horse danced on my foot. It'll be black and blue in the morning."

Morris laughs out loud. "Listen to you, Davy, my boy. You're soft as well as wet nowadays. It wasn't Liege's fault; he just doesn't like the snow and he wanted to get inside."

With this, Ned, who has stripped down to his undergarments, joins in. "Yes, he just wanted to get inside and have something to eat. Come to think of it, I need something to eat."

Alard, alarmed at Ned's state of undress, asks, "I hope that you're going to put something on before we eat?"

"Oh yes, don't worry. I won't excite the serving staff. I just need to get a dry shirt from the bottom of my satchel."

We watch in wonder as Ned removes all manner of items, before dressing himself and repacking his satchel.

Peter, shaking his head in astonishment, questions, "How on earth do you manage to get all that in there?"

Ned laughs. "I'm a genius, that's how."

Laughter fills the air and immediately it feels like old times.

The great hall is accessed via a short internal passageway, and for this we are all eternally grateful as the snow is now coming down thick and fast. Looking through the partially open shutters into the inner bailey, the scene before us looks magical.

Morris is the first to comment. "God be praised that we made it when we did. I should hate to be travelling in this."

I shiver at the very thought of it and silently pray that Pip is safe and warm. Perhaps in a tavern somewhere close by, with a roaring fire and plenty to eat. My stomach rumbles. Embarrassed, I apologise.

Ned loudly announces that he feels exactly the same way. "Oh, how I long for Sunday. I can almost taste the freshly roasted meats."

With this, I wonder what tonight's Holy Thursday meal will consist of. I sincerely hope that that there are no leeks involved, as I've had my fill of them this Lent. As we approach the dais, we are met by a short but rotund man in black robes. He has a kind face and very pale skin. So pale that I can almost see every vein in his hands and neck. I doubt that he is much older than myself, but he appears to be weighed down by the weight of the world.

"Good evening, all. I am Father John de Bocking. Please forgive me for keeping you all waiting. It took an age to prepare and bless the oils, and even longer to wash the altar. My hands are like blocks of ice, but I should not complain as I have been engaged in the Lord's work." Shaking his head, he immediately appears sad. "Please forgive me. I forget my manners. Please come, let me show you to your seats."

As we walk, I notice that Father John continues to rub his hands together, obviously trying to get warm.

Once we are seated, Osbert de Mortimer approaches from the farthest end of the hall. He is accompanied by an elderly man, whose robes are almost as fine as his – the only difference being the colour. Osbert's are dark green and the elderly man's are red. I presume this to be Robert Boydell due to the high-status colour that he is wearing.

Stopping just in front of us, the elderly man looks directly into my eyes, smiles and then lowers his head in a respectful manner before speaking, "Lady Harsyck, I am very pleased to meet you. I am Robert Boydell, a steward of this fine castle. I have known your husband for many years, and I greatly admire his courage, strength and bravery, but more importantly his kind soul."

My heart swells with pride. "Thank you so much for your kind words. Pip is indeed a fine man and a wonderful husband."

I wonder how Robert Boydell knows Pip so well. Perhaps he will tell me more later. My mind then wanders to the vacant seat next to Owain. It is a throne similar to the one that I sat on earlier in the chamber. I can't help but think that this must be Countess Maud's seat.

In keeping with the tradition of the day, Father John now asks us to remove our shoes, for it is time to have our feet washed by him, to replicate the act of Jesus washing his disciples' feet. Well, I say *washed*, it actually feels more like having a wet rag drawn over my feet. I suspect that Father John does not wish to fully immerse his hands in the tepid water and get cold once more.

That done, we are now all ready to eat. This time, it is Owain's stomach that rumbles loudly and, as if by magic, the kitchen door opens and plates of food are bought in by the retainers who I saw earlier in the inner bailey. Noticing that they have changed, I wonder if they, too, have had their feet washed. I doubt it, though, as Jesus only washed twelve pairs of feet and I can't imagine Father John wanting to wash over that number. The food smells incredible and, to my relief, there is not even the slightest essence of leeks. Struggling to make up my mind, I gratefully accept a ladle of sowpres dorry, accompanied by a spoonful of sauce verde and a slice of bread that appears to contain nettle leaves. The sowpres dorry is a warm and comforting soup. Not too thick and not too thin. The onions, although old, are quite mild and the inclusion of white wine, toasted almonds and breadcrumbs makes for a creamy texture. I carefully break off a piece of the nettle bread and dip it into the sauce verde. The bread immediately takes on the colour and flavour of the herbs. Parsley, mint and garlic have all been ground down and mixed with vinegar. I know that this sauce often accompanies poached fish, but as I can smell none, it would seem that we are in for a tasty, but heavily restricted Lenten meal. Carefully placing the soaked bread into the soup, I take pleasure in creating green spirals before tasting it once more. The next remove is even more delicious. Pears have been cooked in red wine and flavoured with ginger. Sated and relaxed, I sit and observe the comings and goings in the hall before saying goodnight to everyone and being accompanied to my first-floor solar chamber by Peter.

"Now, Mistress, if you could just wait here for a few moments, I would like to check your chamber. Conisbrough holds no danger, but the habits of a lifetime are hard to break and I would feel happier checking."

Far from being offended, I am grateful for Peter's diligence.

The chamber is sumptuous and exudes an air of faded grandeur. Yet another throne-like chair takes pride of place next to a very grand fireplace, where a fire burns brightly. The room is incredibly warm and I undress to my linen kirtle. Sitting in the throne, I take in my surroundings. There is a large bed with heavy curtains and a great many cushions, a carved table and chair, which match exactly, and many stained-glass panels in the large solar window. From what I can see, the panels are mainly red, yellow and green glass, but I'll know better in the morning, when the sun rises. Rather than retire to bed, I close my eyes and drift off by the fire.

When I wake, it is morning, and the fire is now a mass of dying embers. I rise and stretch, before walking over to the window. The glass panels are indeed red, yellow and green. I ponder on the significance of the colours. Were they Countess Maud's favourite colours, or do they hold a greater significance? Perhaps they are aligned to her lineage, or maybe the Neville lands that she inherited from her first marriage. Either way, they are very beautiful. However, I feel uncomfortable in this chamber and sense the presence of a restless spirit. Does Maud's spirit roam free, paying penance for her godson's sins? For it was John Clifford who murdered Edmund Earl of Rutland in cold blood. Whatever the reason, I will not sleep in her bed. Perhaps Alard can arrange for me to move chambers tonight.

Not wishing to waste the day, I dress quickly and sit upon the cushioned window seat. The landscape is even more beautiful today. White and pure. However, the silence and my daydream is quickly broken by a familiar knock on the door. I know it to be Peter, as only last night we agreed on a special code that would alert me to him on the other side of the door. As I rise and turn, I am alarmed to catch a glimpse of white mist in the air, which disappears almost immediately. Calling out to Peter, I investigate the garderobe before leaving, but there is no sign of fire or smoke. Perhaps it was Maud's spirit that I saw!

Deciding to keep the vision to myself, I follow Peter to the great hall. Once inside, I am greeted by a sombre scene. Dark linen has been draped over all the tables and the dais in preparation for the Good Friday service. We walk through the hall in silence to the kitchen, where we find everyone seated around a large oval table. After greeting everyone, we sit and listen to the intense conversation between Davy and Alard.

Davy seems agitated. "Well, I think that we have no option but to leave and travel to Warwick Castle. Time is of the essence and if the rolls are to be believed, we have very little time to play with."

Alard appears to be conflicted. "Yes, I agree time is very limited, but the snow appears deep and a little icy in patches. I must have time to consider all of the available options." Turning and walking to the small window, Alard scratches his head before starting again. "The sky looks heavily laden and if it snows again, we may get trapped here for days. I doubt that Freemantle or Liege could cope with the snow being any deeper. You are right, Davy; we will leave straight away, but not for Fotheringhay. We must travel direct to Warwick." Turning to look at me, Alard asks, "Mistress Bethany, are you in agreement?"

My mind returns to Duke Richard's cold and frozen body, which lies lifeless at Pontefract Castle. "Yes, Alard, I agree. We must make haste and do what we must. Ned, please can you walk with me so that I can fetch my belongings? And then you can tell me what you have found within the rolls." With that, I drink a cup of small beer and prepare to leave.

Inside the safety of the chamber, Ned hesitates before speaking, "I do not like this chamber – the air is cold and damp. Was it like this last night? If so, I will complain to Robert Boydell. You should not have had to sleep in conditions like this." Turning, Ned notices the bed is still made. "Mistress Bethany, did you make the bed yourself this morning?"

Shaking my head, I tell Ned how I slept in the chair by the roaring fire last night and did not wake until morning, when the fire had all but gone out. "No one has mentioned anything, but from the location and the status of the contents, I believe this could be Countess Maud's chamber and, if so, I could not sleep in her bed. She may have been the stepmother of Duke Richard, but she was also the aunt and godmother of John Clifford. She would have known him since birth, when he was born in this very castle – maybe even in this very chamber." I stop and shudder violently. "I could not rest where she had lain."

Ned nods in agreement. "Well, that would account for the bad feeling in my gut then."

Walking over to the solar window, we sit side by side.

"Well, Ned, what have you found?"

"Ah well, this is a very sensitive matter. It would appear that Duke Richard may have been in negotiations with John Talbot, the first Earl of Shrewsbury and Waterford, a few years ago regarding the betrothal of his eldest son, now King Edward, to John Talbot's daughter, Lady Eleanor Talbot. This, in itself, would have been a highly desirable match when Edward was the Earl of March, but not now that he is king. Warwick was furious when he was informed of the negotiations by one of Talbot's sons. He has now stated openly that he is the only nobleman worthy of advising the king. He is also intent on grasping as much power and land as possible. He's gone mad, crazy and, worst of all, dangerous. We suspect that if the king will not bend to Warwick's will, then he may well change his allegiance to Queen Margaret of Anjou. It all began when Duke Richard rightly claimed the throne of England. Warwick was furious with his uncle for claiming the throne, and even more furious with his father for supporting Richard. Then, a series of blazing rows ensued with both Edmund and Edward intervening to stop them. Then, when the Act of Accord was finally decided upon, Warwick was furious at having to pay out vast sums of money to John Clifford in damages, before the final insult of having to walk behind his father and the Duke of Somerset, and alongside the Duke of Exeter, to St Paul's Cathedral on the Loveday."

Struggling to take this all in, I try to recall the missives that I read while living at South Acre. I can remember Pip's anxiety all too well, but to be honest, I can remember little else as everything was changing at such an alarming speed.

I try to vocalise my concerns. "So, Ned, is the problem Eleanor Talbot or Warwick's ambitions?"

"To be honest, both, but if we can prevent Edward and Eleanor's betrothal becoming official, it would solve a great many problems down the line, as a more advantageous marriage may be possible."

In my innocence, I ask, "Do Eleanor and Edward know one another?"

"Oh yes, and Edward is besotted by Eleanor. She is known to possess a beauty most rare. So, you see, if we can prevent the betrothal, and Warwick can assume the position of chief adviser and confident to Edward, then he will be content and disaster will be averted. Well, for now, anyway."

"You say 'for now' – is there something else?"

Scratching his head, Ned looks extremely concerned. "Yes. We think so. We have heard rumours of a kidnap plot." Noting the horror on my face, Ned continues, "Not Edward – in a way, it's far worse – but his younger brothers, George and Richard."

Wanting to know more, I nod my head in Ned's direction, too stunned for words.

"Well, they're on their way back from the Burgundian Court to England for Edward's coronation and are due to set sail any day soon. For all we know, they may even be crossing the sea as we speak. Naturally, we have lookouts both in France and all along the south coast of England, but this may not be enough. Thomas Stanley and his men are up to their old tricks again and, Bethany, what I am about to say will be hard for you to hear. About ten years ago, Stanley was instructed by King Henry to imprison Duke Richard upon his return from Ireland within the mighty walls of Conway Castle, and to execute Sir William Oldhall immediately upon apprehension."

Unable to control myself, I let out a howl of pain. "They planned to kill my uncle!"

"Yes, Bethany, to kill him without a trial. Make no mistake; we are dealing with evil people, who have no morals and think only of themselves. Death means nothing to them, and if they can murder George and Richard, then only Edward remains between the Lancastrians and their ambitions to reclaim the throne."

The thought of all that murder chills me to the bone.

After a period of silence, Ned continues, "There is not a moment to lose, Bethany. We must make haste to Warwick Castle and establish your place within the household. It will not seem out of place if we can arrive within the next week or so, as Warwick Castle is being used as a meeting place for all those who travel to Edward's coronation from the north."

Needing to know more, I quiz Ned about those that I will meet at Warwick.

"Ah, yes… well, this is where it all gets a bit tricky and somewhat like a spider's web. Eleanor Neville, wife to Thomas Stanley, Earl of Derby, will be in residence, as she is the sister of Richard, Earl of Warwick. She's officially known as Lady Eleanor Stanley. Her allegiances appear to be aligned to those of her brother and not her husband, but no one really knows. Her marriage to Thomas Stanley does not appear to have been a love match, although it has given life to three babes in arms – Thomas, Alice and George – within the last two years. All of whom travel with her at all times. Rumour has it that she fears her husband's family taking them away from her and bringing them up in isolation at their manors of Knowsley, Lathom or Burscough. We have heard that Lady Eleanor Stanley grieves for her father, Richard, Earl of Salisbury; her uncle, Duke Richard; and her other relatives that were cut down at Wakefield."

"If this is true, then surely she is one of us?"

"Alas, Bethany, we cannot tell at the moment," Ned replies. "Lady Stanley and her children will lodge at their

London home of Derby House at St Paul's Wharf to await the coronation. Then, we have the Countess of Warwick, Anne Beauchamp, who is travelling to Warwick Castle from her northern home of Middleham Castle. She travels with her two daughters, Isabel and Anne, and Margaret, Warwick's illegitimate daughter."

Initially shocked to hear of Warwick's illegitimate daughter, I long to hear more about her.

"Margaret is the eldest of all of Warwick's children and it is thought that her mother was from the Marcher area between England and Wales. I hear that she is dearly loved by everyone and that she has a sweet temperament. Warwick Castle was once the seat of Richard Earl of Salisbury and is now the main residence of the Beauchamp family. Anne's sister, Elizabeth, is married to John Talbot, second Earl of Shrewsbury and Waterford – and, yes, I can note from the recognition in your eyes that it is the son of John Talbot who negotiated with Duke Richard about the possible union between Eleanor and Edward."

Suddenly, the penny drops and I can see what I need to do. I need to gain everyone's trust and ascertain loyalties and divisions.

I ask Ned, "Will there be others of note at Warwick Castle?"

"Yes, Lady Willoughby. Maud Stanhope, wife to the late Thomas Neville, is making her way to Warwick from Sherriff Hutton Castle in North Yorkshire. Recently widowed, Lady Willoughby bristles with hatred at those who killed her much-loved husband and her father-in-law, Richard, Earl of Salisbury."

With not a moment to lose, I rise and pack my belongings into my trunk and satchel. Sad not to have had the opportunity to explore the castle more, I state my intention to return once the task in hand is complete. However, as we leave the chamber, the swirling white mist returns, and this time it is accompanied by a strong gust of wind. So strong that the bed curtains are sent in all different directions. Perhaps I won't return, after all!

To Worksop Castle with All Speed

"Here we go again," says Morris, laughing. "Let's hope the snow holds off until nightfall, although I doubt that it will."

Alard, who appears slightly prickly, asks Morris to be more positive.

To this request Morris just leans into me and laughs. "Well, this is a welcome change of plan. I can't say that I relished the thought of cutting across country from Fotheringhay to Warwick. The fields in that part can get water-logged in a matter of hours, and the clay, well, that sticks to everything. At this time of year, I much prefer to ride from Worksop to Nottingham, then Leicester to Leamington Prior and beyond to Warwick. It's a much more comfortable journey, too. For the most part, all of the roads follow the ancient Roman ones. Of course, they've been made good and upgraded over the years, but the routes have never really changed. When I was a boy, we used to find Roman coins and green glass bottles every time the fields were ploughed or the roads dug up."

Shaking the reins and looking at the sky, Morris looks pensive. I suspect that the impending snow worries everyone.

Morris begins again, "We'll be stopping at Laughton en le Morthen and Throapham on the way to Worksop. Both are lovely little hamlets with good ale houses. Freemantle and Liege will be able to rest their weary legs there before the last leg to Worksop."

Ned begins to laugh manically. "Oh, Morris, you make me cry with laughter! You mean that *you* can rest there. I seem to recall that a rather top-heavy wench that you are rather keen on lives at Throapham."

To this, everyone laughs.

Morris, seeing the funny side of Ned's comments, also begins to roll around in laughter. "Ah… I suspect that you are talking about Mistress Honey Morton, the brewer at the White Lion Inn, Throapham. Yes, she's a grand woman. A widow with her own mind and the best honeyed brew that I've ever tasted. Apart from that, I've never noticed anything else about her."

The laughter grows even louder, as Morris's face turns increasingly pink with embarrassment.

To save Morris, I seek to change the subject. "Please tell me more about the Roman roads."

A relieved-looking Morris happily obliges. "Well, the first Roman road that we'll travel by is known as the Fosse Way and then, at High Cross, we'll turn right onto Watling Street."

Nodding my head, I consider the names. 'Watling Street' I already know of, but 'Fosse Way' – what could that mean? "Morris, what does 'Fosse Way' mean?"

"Ah well, 'Fosse' means ditch, and in the olden days the Fosse Way was a deep ditch that ran from Exeter at one end of the country to Leicester at the other, with further ditches branching out on either side to places like Lincoln and Cirencester. These ditches were dug by the Romans and acted as borders. A very physical indication that the Romans had not only invaded but that they were now in control."

I shudder at the thought of a foreign invader, and especially at the thought of the Romans. I consider the place name 'Cirencester' for a moment. Somewhere in the back of my mind, Cirencester seems to ring a bell.

"Ah, Mistress Bethany, I can see that something has caught your attention."

"Yes, Morris, I'm sure that I've heard of Cirencester before."

"That you have, Mistress. Not only does our dear Davy come from down that way, but Duke Richard held the manor of Bisley close by. It came to him through his uncle, Edmund, the Earl of March, and it's part of the Mortimer inheritance."

"Yes, I remember now. Just before we left Towton Hall, King Edward mentioned that he had received a letter from the townspeople of Cirencester, asking for permission to honour his father by creating a life-size stained-glass image of him. I believe that they wanted to install it within the parish church of St John the Baptist, so that all can come and pay their respects and light candles in Duke Richard's memory."

"You've got a good memory, Mistress Bethany. That's exactly what was said."

Looking up at the sky, I contemplate the large snowflakes, which are beginning to fall at an alarming rate, before noticing that Morris is now holding onto the reins of Liege and Freemantle even tighter than before. Without speaking,

Ned, Alard, Owain and Peter have positioned themselves, one at each corner of the cart, while Davy is walking in front of Liege and Freemantle.

Morris, noting my concern, wipes the snow from his eyes and tries to comfort me. "There's no need to worry, Mistress Bethany. We're nearly there now. We've just got to make sure that we don't slide, as the snow and ice can cause havoc with the wheels."

In the distance, we all breathe a sigh of relief as the tiny hamlets of Laughton en le Morthen and Throapham come into view. Nestling close to each other, it's hard to believe that they are sperate entities.

Ned calls out from the rear of the cart, "God be praised! We're nearly there now and I can almost taste the ale and the hot pies on offer in the White Lion Inn."

Alard, as cautious as ever, calls out, "Yes, we're nearly there now, but please be careful, and don't take your mind off the job in hand. From memory, there's a deep ditch surrounding the hamlets, and the ancient well under Throapham church often floods the surrounding fields. We must be careful of unseen icy patches."

Alas, no sooner than those words are spoken, Davy crashes to the ground with a sickening scream. "Help! Help! My ankle!"

Bringing the cart to a steady halt, Ned rushes to Davy's side, closely followed by the others. "Let me help you. What happened? Did you slip?"

To my frustration, I am unable to see Davy, until he is lifted up in a joint effort. "That bloody horse – he knocked me over."

Morris, taking offence, responds, "Don't swear about Liege like that. He's a horse and he doesn't mean any harm.

He must have stood on a sharp stone or something. He'd never normally swing his head around like that." Climbing down, Morris attends to Liege, as Davy is lifted into the back of the cart and covered with an old sack to keep him warm. "Well, I never, come over here, Alard, and look at this."

Alard, concerned at Morris's beckoning, walks swiftly to Liege's side, and after inspecting all of Liege's legs for abrasions or blood, he bends down. "Oh my word."

Intrigue and frustration fills the air before Owain bellows out, "What is it? What have you found?"

Alard, now standing, holds up an extremely large livery badge before noting, "I expect this was the reason that Liege danced around and knocked you over, Davy. It's as sharp as a knife."

Unable to hold my thoughts any longer, I ask, "Can you recognise the livery? Who does it belong to?"

An extremely alarmed Alard looks around and rubs his head. "If I'm not mistaken, it belongs to Thomas Stanley."

A collective gasp fills the air before Peter rushes to Alard's side and gently takes the badge from Alard's open hand. Holding it up, he shakes his head in what looks like anger. Inspecting every detail, he acknowledges that it is the three-legged device from Thomas Stanley's crest. "Yes, I recognise this device all too well. The legs represent the Stanley claim to the Kingdom of Mann. An island just off the north-west coast of England, which sits perilously close to Ireland. This deluded man fashions himself as the King of Mann and throws his weight around freely. How I despise him. I would run him through with a blade as soon as look at him. He sought the death of Duke Richard and Sir William Oldhall and created no end of problems for the Duke with some of the more fanatical Irish Lords. God curse him and his family."

"Does this mean that Stanley and his men are in the vicinity?" I ask.

Worried for our safety, Alard calls Ned and Owain to his side. "That's exactly what I was thinking. We can't stay out here all night, but, equally, we cannot risk entering the hamlets without knowing who is there."

Immediately, Peter speaks, "That's an easy problem to deal with. We'll push the cart deep into the tree line and light a fire close by. The trees will both shelter and camouflage us, and the fire will provide warmth and allow us to cook. Fearing that we may not always be able to stay at inns, I took the liberty of bringing a barrel of ale and a box of supplies. We have bread, cheese, bacon and pies aplenty."

Alard, smiling, announces that he did the same, but chose not to say anything as he did not want to cause alarm.

After waving goodbye to Peter and wishing him a safe and speedy return, all hands set about creating two shelters. The first for Liege and Freemantle, and the second for us. Determined to help, I climb down from the cart and help to unroll an extremely large piece of waxed linen. I presume that it must be of a great age, as it is stained and smells of smoke. Owain, using his blade, fashions four uprights from the branches of a nearby oak tree, while Ned does the same. Morris unrolls eight lengths of seasoned rope before digging eight post holes. In no time at all, both canopies are erected and we are ensconced in the warm and dry. Sharing our space with Liege and Freemantle, we all sit on a bed of straw, which Freemantle proceeds to eat. Laughing at his antics, we all rest until we hear Peter make his presence known.

"We're safe. Mistress Morten says that Stanley and his men passed through the hamlets about fourteen days ago and that they were heading north. We can proceed to the White Lion Inn at our leisure. Mistress Morten is preparing our accommodation as I speak."

Sighs of relief are quickly overtaken by Ned's laughter. "Mistress Morten, eh… she's preparing your bed, Morris. I wonder if she is preparing herself, too."

With these words, laughter breaks the silence and Morris's blushes are covered by the impending dusk.

After eating all of the pies, packing away the canopies, putting out the fire and preparing Liege and Freemantle for the final part of the journey, Davy once again leads the way. This time, though, with more care to keep at an arm's length from Liege. Owain, as optimistic as ever, considers the possibility of a few games of dice with Ned.

Alard sighs. "Lads, you know what Pip would say to that, don't you? Surely he would frown upon it."

Ned, however, cheekily points out that Pip would agree to a few games of dice, as long as information is gleaned from the locals.

Begrudgingly, Alard agrees to three games of dice. "Alright, but only three games, you hear me, and no strong ale."

This appears to please everyone and we move on at a pace.

The White Lion is a warm and friendly inn with wood panelling and a roaring fire. I look around at the pale-blue walls and notice that the stools have been fashioned from pieces of aged oak. Each has a cushioned seat, with not a single stain in sight. Fresh rushes cover the floor and the room smells of sweet sage and thyme. On the furthest wall hangs an exact copy of the Mortimer shield. I immediately feel at home and begin to relax. Seated on a stool by the fire, I await our host. Within a few minutes, the curtain is drawn back across the door to reveal a most handsome woman. Ignoring convention, her thick red hair tumbles loose about her shoulders and her breasts. Shocked to see such a low-cut kirtle, I attempt to avert my eyes, but to no avail. Surely this is Honey Morton.

Bobbing down politely before me, Honey attempts to curtsy before taking my hands in hers. "Welcome, Mistress Bethany. I have heard of you many times before and I am so pleased to meet you."

Honey has a soft, gentle voice and appears childlike – untouched by the evils of the outside world. I wonder how Honey has heard of me, but then I remember Morris.

Honey continues, "You know my mother, Alice. She was your travelling companion when you left your home of Stratfield Mortimer."

Looking into Honey's eyes once more, I see the resemblance and smile. "Dear Alice; how is she? Is she here?"

"Oh yes, she's upstairs finishing off your room." Laughing, Honey exclaims that we'll hear her mother approach before we see her. To this, we all laugh.

As anticipated, we hear Alice approach before we see her. True to form, she is berating a young maid for not having cleaned the floor to her exacting standards. "Now, come along, Molly, no sloughing is allowed. I want that floor to shine like the sun before I retire to bed."

Morris, having been absent in the stables, putting Liege and Freemantle to bed, enters the inn at exactly the same time that Alice can be heard bellowing. Rolling his eyes, he calls out, "Is that Alice I hear?"

Honey answers, "Yes, that's Alice. My mother is out the back; she'll be through in a moment."

Morris, in a state of confusion, looks around at a sea of laughing faces. "*Mother*? What do you mean *mother*?"

Honey, now looking as confused as Morris, smiles and confirms that Alice Mowbray is, indeed, her mother. "Do you know her, Morris?"

This is accompanied by even louder laughter as Morris goes white and says, "Oh yes, I know your mother and have done so for many a year, but I never realised that you were her daughter."

By the look on Morris's face, I can only imagine that he's thinking that he's had a lucky escape, for if he had been in a romantic relationship with Honey, Alice might become his mother-in-law, without him knowing until the wedding day.

As Alice enters, she looks directly at Morris. "Morris, you old dog, you. I hope that you haven't been trying to sweet talk my Honey."

Morris, having regained his composure, replies, "Alice, you old bag, it's been a long time and it's good to see you, but you can stop your carrying-on now. You're no match for me."

Looking around the room, it's good to see so much happiness.

The morning comes all too soon and, after breaking our fast, it's time to leave. Owain and Ned – content at playing three games of dice – have cleaned out the cart and are in the process of packing everything neatly back into place. Davy is having balm rubbed into his foot by Molly, and Alard is mending the sole of his boot with a leather patch. Peter is overseeing the supplies and buying more ale for the next part of the journey, while Morris is cleaning the horses' reins and leathers straps in the bright sunshine, which is thawing out some of the snow.

I decide to explore the inn and go in search of Honey and Alice. When I find them, they are sitting in the kitchen, while two young boys turn a huge spit of what looks like lamb over the fire. Both stand as I walk in, then hug me, before we all sit.

Alice, as ever, is the first to speak. "Now, Mistress Bethany, I hope that you are packed and prepared for your journey to Worksop. How I love that castle. It's too sad that I can't join you, but we'll meet again in Warwick. I have to stay here with Honey for the next couple of days. Those Stanley men passed through this way a couple of weeks ago, and I'm concerned that they'll return to seek out my beautiful girl, and if they do, they'll have me to deal with."

This remark makes me long for my mother. She was kind and loving, and feisty, too. I also think of my mother-in-law and hope that she is safe. If only I could hear from Pip, it would put my mind at rest. I try not to linger on that thought, though, as I know that sadness will overcome me if I think about Pip for too long, and I need to keep a clear head.

After sharing a cup of heavily watered wine, I say farewell to Honey and Alice. Outside, everyone awaits and I climb aboard the cart, next to Morris.

Morris, in a high mood, waves in an exaggerated fashion towards Alice and Honey. "Farewell and keep safe. I fear for the Stanley men if they should return – Alice, your tongue will cut them like a knife."

Alice, not to be outdone, waves back and calls out, "Mistress Bethany, I hope that the smell of horse dung fades from Morris shortly."

With laughter all around, we pull away and head towards Worksop Castle.

Leaving Throapham, we pass through Laughton en le Morthen, where a fine castle abuts an extremely large churchyard. I can see row upon row of wooden crosses and freshly covered graves.

Surprised to see so many, I ask, "Morris, why are there so many new graves here?"

His one-word reply chills me. "Towton."

I can't explain why. After all, Towton was a bloody and deadly battle. Perhaps it's the distance from the battlefield that I'm shocked about.

Not wanting to upset the happy mood of the day, I ask Morris if he knows anything about the castle and the adjacent church. "Ay… they're both fine specimens, built on ancient foundations, I'm told. People around here say that they were both built by Edwin, Earl of Mercia, hundreds of years ago and then enlarged. See over there, that fine portcullis and porch, and over there, the steeple tower of the church, with embattlements, crockets and pinnacles. Constructed of limestone and lined with sandstone. I just don't know how they did it. The masons must have had skills way ahead of their times, as the limestone has been cut and shaped exquisitely." Morris scratches his head as he considers. "Perhaps the masons were on loan from the mighty York Minster, as the church is under their control."

"Oh, Morris, how I long to see York Minster."

"Well, Mistress, perhaps when your task is complete, and King Edwards sits safely upon the throne, we will visit the mighty York Minster together. You never know, Pip may be able to join us."

I bask in the happy glow of the future. A time when Pip will be by my side and allow the beauty of the day to inspire me. Leaving Laughton, we pass a wedge-shaped stone arch that is surrounded by decorated panels of chevrons and lozenges, a variety of buildings – one of which I think is a warehouse – and a fine stone wall with an embedded grave cover.

Having never seen the latter before, I ask Morris, "Morris, please could we slow down a little? I long to see that grave cover in closer detail."

"You wish is my command, Mistress."

With a smile, Morris brings the cart to a stop and Ned takes my hand.

"Come, Mistress Bethany, let me take you over to the wall. The snow has fallen onto layers of ice and it may be slippery."

Gratefully, I accept Ned's offer. At the wall, I bend and stretch a little to touch the gravestone. To my surprise, it's almost entirely worn smooth, presumably from the weather, but if I try really hard, I can just about detect deeply incised lines that run around the entire slab. I feel for a name, but there is none. How strange. On further inspection, I can see the same chevron and lozenge pattern that adorns the wedge-shaped stone arch we have just passed. Perhaps this was the family emblem? Climbing back on board the cart, we move off, passing through an impressive gateway.

Towards us flock a long line of people, all dressed in what looks like their Sunday best. Of course, it's Easter Day! How could I have forgotten? I can hear handbells ringing behind us and much joy in people's voices as they pass.

Owain calls out, "Thank God for Easter! We can eat eggs and cheese now."

Alard responds, "Owain, Easter Day is far more than that. Do you only think of your stomach?"

Ned joins in. "Yes, Owain, it's far more than eggs and cheese. There'll be roast meat aplenty at Worksop Castle."

I note from Alard's face that he has no intention of answering the latter. Instead, he asks Morris to up the tempo. "Well, the sooner we get to Worksop, the better then."

Arriving at Worksop

The last few miles to Worksop are the prettiest by far, with the snow clinging to the branches of the trees that line the route, and tiny hamlets with smoke dancing above the roofs. As we approach Worksop, the terrain becomes peppered with rivulets and streams. I can hear the fast-rushing water of the River Ryton ahead. I expect that somewhere upstream the snow is beginning to melt. Davy, raising one hand, signals for Morris to bring Liege and Freemantle to a halt. Alard, no doubt mindful of the many bridges that have collapsed in the past, asks that we cross the wooden bridge in pairs, with Morris, Liege and Freemantle crossing last.

Once over and reunited, I sit in the cart and gaze up at the castle. Dominating the skyline, the stone appears to be almost as white as the snow; with the afternoon sunlight casting hues of gold and red on it, it could almost be on fire. Confused to have turned a sharp right, I am awestruck by the priory gatehouse that sits before me. Glinting as white as the castle, I believe that it must be constructed of the same stone. With a high wall, running all the way around the perimeter of the priory, the gatehouse has the look of a grand hall with a central doorway. The upper level is symmetrical with deep inset windows on either side. Both are glazed with blue and green glass panels, while the lower level is not symmetrical at all. To the left of the large wooden doors is one small window, and to the right is a large arched window in front of what looks like a chapel, which, again, is glazed with blue and green glass panels. This window has niches on either side of it and one centrally positioned above it. The saints are easy to identify. To the left is St Augustine of Hippo; to the right, St Cuthbert; and above, the Virgin Mary. Beneath them, and either side of the wooden gates, there are two more niches. This time, they hold figures of knights. I wonder who they are? Are they just symbolical, protecting the priory? Or perhaps they are knights who are connected in some way. I make a mental note to find out more.

Inside, I can hear the monks chanting and the bells ringing. Alard strides forward purposely and produces a roll of parchment from his satchel. Knocking on the door, he waits until a much smaller, and largely concealed, door is opened.

"Morris, are we to lodge within the priory?"

"Yes, Mistress, the castle is and has always been a Lancastrian stronghold, whereas the priory is loyal to the House of York. Prior Michael was a friend of Duke Richard, and he sheltered both Duke Richard and his supporters after the Battle of Worksop."

"The Battle of Worksop? Morris, I have never heard of this. Please tell me more."

"Well, it wasn't really a battle – more of a skirmish. Duke Richard, the Earl of Salisbury, and many hundreds of troops were making their way north to Sandal Castle, when they were forced to take a detour off the Great North Road, through Worksop. No one really knows why, as both would have known that the town was loyal to the House of Lancaster. It may have been the weather – there was terrible flooding last year – or it could have been that they were running short of supplies, and it is widely known that there is a fine market in Worksop every Thursday, or it could have been to meet up with more supporters. Whatever the reason, they were cornered and trapped on the morning of the 16th December by troops loyal to the Duke of Somerset."

Hearing that name, my blood begins to boil over and my face burns red in anger. Somerset – how I despise that man!

"To my knowledge, very few died, and the ones that did were Somerset's men. I have heard that one skull, with a bodkin arrowhead lodged firmly within it, rests within the priory church, as a warning of the evils that surround the town. Rumour has it that Somerset leaves his men to rot where they fall."

Even with my hatred of Somerset, I have some feeling for his troops, who are misused. No one should be left to rot where they fall.

I am jolted back to the present as Liege and Freemantle move forward. Entering through the large wooden doors, I am taken aback by the beauty within. Monks are hard at work preparing what looks like alms for the locals, with many appearing wet-through after picking fresh nettles and herbs from the neatly tended beds, which sit at the base of the stone walls. Others supervise great cauldrons of steaming pottage over open fires. Owain and Ned look concerned.

"Owain, can you see what I can see? I hope that nettle pottage isn't for us. I need meat."

Owain, shaking his head in agreement with Ned, can't hide his disappointment. "I hope that isn't for us either. I'm fed up of pottage, and nettles have never been a favourite of mine."

A laughing Morris puts both of their minds at rest. "Lads, I'm sure that there'll be meat aplenty – you forget that we are the protectors of Lady Bethany Harsyck, a most revered lady, who travels to Warwick on the king's business. The House of the Augustines will most surely cater for us, as they cater for all, whether they are rich or poor. Did you not see the accommodation room set aside within the gatehouse for weary travellers and the pilgrims who make their way to the Shrine of the Virgin Mary?"

Nodding their heads, they can see Morris's logic.

Longing to know more, I cannot help but ask, "Morris, the Shrine of the Virgin Mary, is that behind the arched window, which is glazed with blue and green glass?"

"Yes, that's right. They have their own shrine here. No one knows who really founded it, but I expect that it was one of the Furnival family. Their tombs are a sight to behold in the priory church dedicated to St Mary. Thomas Furnival's tomb depicts him as a knight and is known to be jewel-encrusted. Founding a shrine on the doorstep of a king's highway makes perfect economic sense, even if I'm a little unbelieving about their real motives."

I cross myself immediately and gently reprimand Morris for being so cynical.

"Ay… you're right, Mistress. I'm a bad boy to say such things."

Although, in all honesty, I doubt that Morris feels any sense of sorrow at saying such things, as he laughs while apologising.

Rounding the corner, past the cloisters, we are met by Prior Michael, who stands upright with the use of a staff. I try not to stare at his back and arm, as they are very deformed. Climbing down from the cart, Prior Michael unexpectedly bows before me.

Alarmed at this, and concerned that he will lose his balance, I immediately take his hand and squeeze it. "Good day, Prior Michael, it's very good to meet you."

With this, Prior Michael straightens up as much as possible. "Lady Harsyck, I am honoured to meet you. Duke Richard spoke of you when he last visited." We both immediately cross ourselves and struggle to contain our tears. "Duke Richard was a good friend of mine. I had known him and your uncle, Sir William Oldhall, for many a year. When I was young, I accompanied Duke Richard to Calais on many occasions."

Knowing nothing of this period, I see an opportunity to learn more. "Prior Michael, oh how I would love to hear your reminisces about your adventures in France. I have never been and probably never shall."

"Of course, my dear, I would love to revisit my memories. Perhaps after our meal would be a good time."

We both nod and smile, before I reboard the cart and we move forward towards the accommodation, which is set behind the priory church.

Passing the cloisters, we encounter yet more monks tending raised beds of herbs and vegetables, and a great many outside ovens, from which great plumes of smoke escape. The smell of bread cooking is delicious. Racks of pastries sit upon wooden tables, waiting their turn within the ovens. Food is being prepared in great quantities. This will surely be an Easter feast to remember. Owain and Ned soon realise that their fears are unfounded, as there are at least ten spits of meat on the go, each sheltered beneath a wooden canopy. Arriving at the door to the hall, I wait patiently until I am invited to climb down. I must remember that I am now a lady and on the king's business. It hurts to think that I have to act in a certain way, especially when Alard, Ned, Davy, Peter, Owain and Morris are all so dear to me, but lives are at stake.

Inside the priory church of St Mary, I am astounded by the decoration, as it's just so beautiful! Greenery laced with pale blue, white and green silk ribbons adorn each altar and windowsill. The font that stands before me has also been decorated and, to my delight, there is a small reconstruction of Jesus's empty tomb at the foot of the font. The detail is amazing. Not only can I see inside the tomb, but there are swathes of cloth and a large rock to one side. I cross myself and say a silent prayer before moving on.

Surprisingly, Prior Michael turns and leads us out of the priory church, down a narrow gravel pathway, towards the guest accommodation and smiles. "Provision has been made for all of you. You will each have a private room with washing facilities tonight. A large bowl and fresh linen has already been placed in each room; all you need to do is to ring the bell at the end of the corridor and jugs of hot water will be provided. I understand that tomorrow you will be leaving early to journey to Clipstone, therefore I will make sure that bread, cheese and watered ale is left by your doors at first light. An early start is a very good idea, especially as men loyal to the Duke of Somerset have been seen in the area. My sources have told me that they are heading towards Hull in the east, so you should be safe, but just to make sure, I have arranged that the baggage train of Lady Eleanor Talbot will draw into the courtyard to collect you. I think that from now on you should always travel in a large party. Crossing the country is a dangerous pursuit. Manors are far more polarised in their allegiances in the middle-lands. Alard tells me that you will rest at Nottingham Castle, before travelling to Leicester, then Leamington Priors via High Cross and eventually Warwick. In my opinion, this is the safest and most direct route. I myself travel this route every time I visit Ludlow, and I always travel with a high-status baggage train. In the most, thieves and vagabonds are extremely wary of baggage trains and, more importantly, the heavily weaponed retainers that travel with them."

My head begins to spin. "Prior Michael, would you mind awfully if I rest in my room a little before exploring any further?"

"Of course, Lady Harsyck. I'll take you to your room immediately, but please can I enquire if you are ill, or if there is anything that I can get for you?"

"No, not ill, just a little dizzy."

Immediately, Ned and Peter are by my side. Ned, looking concerned, takes my arm. "Lady Harsyck, please let me and Peter accompany you to your room."

Nodding gratefully, we follow Prior Michael up the spiral staircase, before stopping at a large wooden door.

"Lady Harsyck, please allow me to unlock your door for you and then I will leave you in the safe hands of your retainers, as I need to oversee the Easter Day plans."

"Thank you, Prior Michael, I hope to rejoin you shortly."

My room is spartan but clean. There is a bed with fresh linen, a stool and a small table. On the table sits a large brown bowl and strips of linen, while above hangs a crucifix upon the wall. Peter, sensing that I long to speak to Ned, smiles before taking up a defensive position just outside of my door and pulls it shut with one huge tug. The hinges creak loudly as it closes. I sit on my bed, while Ned moves the stool closer and takes a seat.

"Bethany, are you ill?"

"No, Ned, I just wanted to speak to you alone and I could think of no other way to shake off Prior Michael. He has said so many things that have alarmed me and I need to deal with each one in turn."

A smiling Ned relaxes. "Well, if you don't mind me saying, that was an excellent plan. Now, let's deal with each thing in order."

"Well, let's start with Lady Eleanor Talbot's baggage train. Do we know where Lady Talbot has been or where she is going?"

To this, Ned scratches his head. "My guess would be that she has been staying with the king at Towton Hall, under the guise of protection."

I consider the king and Eleanor and wonder if they are lovers. Something that I would never say out loud for fear of being overheard.

"Then, I suspect that she is on her way to Warwick Castle via friendly manors. Perhaps she will also travel with us to London for Edward's coronation."

To this, I also scratch my head and wonder whether Eleanor may even sit next to King Edward upon the dais before their betrothal is announced. Surely not, for this would cause a furore.

Ned, reading my thoughts, steps in, "I also wonder if they are to announce their betrothal and how this will be accepted. Then, Prior Michael mentioned Somerset's men, and the fact that the manors in the middle-lands tend to be more polarised." Ned brushes a hair from his tunic and smiles. "We have nothing to worry about in that respect; we know our enemies and have them under surveillance."

Feeling a little more reassured, I tackle my final worry. "I wonder why Prior Michael frequently travels to Ludlow and how he has such close ties with Lady Talbot's retinue."

A very relaxed-looking Ned leans over. "You've got the making of a fantastic spy, Bethany. You take nothing for granted and you examine everything closely." With this, he chuckles. "Prior Michael is also a Yorkist spy and he travels the route regularly, ingratiating himself with all and alienating none. He has particularly close links with the Talbot family due to their patronage of the priory, although, in truth, they are a little strained recently as the Talbot family now have mixed allegiances. The reason he gives to all for travelling is always the same – he is collecting rents along the way."

With these words of comfort, I relax and consider Easter once more. "Ned, let's rejoin the others now and explore the priory. Morris has told me of a jewel-encrusted tomb that I would love to see."

Ned smiles, stands bolt upright and calls to Peter, "Peter, we are ready to leave and participate in the Easter festivities."

The door opens wide with a deep crunching sound and we all leave in search of Sir Thomas Furnival's tomb.

Entering the priory church once more, we are joined by Alard and Davy. I suspect that Morris and Owain are tending to the needs of Liege and Freemantle in the stables. Towards the end of the central aisle, by the main altar, we can see candles flickering and monks kneeling. We walk silently in the direction of the candlelight. As we get closer, I can see that the monks are decorating the base of a large stone tomb. As we approach, they stand and brush down their habits before welcoming us with outstretched hands and stepping back.

It's at this point that I catch my first full glimpse of the tomb of Sir Thomas Furnival. The stone, almost white in colour, appears to be completely smooth. Sir Thomas's stone effigy, which lays on top of the tomb, is dressed in elaborate robes. The folds of the fabric have been intricately carved and his stone belt is encrusted with real jewels. Pearls and rubies sit alongside sapphires and emeralds. I just cannot begin to imagine the value of the tomb or the security that is needed to protect it.

Owain, noting my shock, steps forward and whispers in my ear, "The tomb is watched over day and night. Don't look around, but there are monks positioned in the upper gallery, and I'm certain that they have small bows and arrows with them."

I long to turn around and look, but I decide to avert my eyes and proceed to the high altar. Kneeling, I say a prayer for my Pip and long that he was here with me to celebrate Easter.

Inside the great hall, the majority of the long wooden tables have been scrubbed and decorated in a modest manner. However, the top table is a sight to behold. Large white candles sit side by side with enamelled glassed and pewter plates. The priory's treasures have been brought out for the feast and it would seem that others are expected. Prior Michael, entering through a side door, smiles and approaches us. After exchanging a few unheard words with Alard, I am led to the top table, while the others are shown to the long wooden table in the middle of the room. I take my seat, sink into the deep cushions and watch as the room fills up. It would seem that no expense has been spared.

Outside, I can hear the sound of carts drawing to a halt and a great many people. Prior Michael swiftly leaves the hall, closely followed by four monks. When he returns, he is accompanied by two ladies. The first is tall and slim, and dressed from head to toe in brown linen. At her waist is a plain kirtle and in her hand is a leather satchel, very similar to that of my mother's old satchel. She has a look of concern on her face and, from her demeanour, I believe her to be a lady-in-waiting. Behind her follows the sweetest and most beautiful lady that I have ever seen in my life. She is very petite with large brown eyes and a tiny waist. Her kirtle consists of emerald-green and sapphire-blue woollen panels, and her girdle is decorated with pewter suns and stars.

I stand to greet both ladies. Prior Michael, having overtaken them, introduces me as Lady Philip Harsyck. Both smile and curtsy. In turn, I do the same before Prior Michael introduces them. "Lady Harsyck, please let me introduce Lady Eleanor Talbot and her lady-in-waiting, Eva de Mortain."

To my surprise, Eleanor reaches out and takes my hand, her tiny fingers clasping mine tightly. "Lady Harsyck, Bethany, I believe." Even more surprised to hear her speak my name, I quiver a little and nod. "The king has spoken of you a great deal and I had the great pleasure of meeting your husband at Towton Hall."

Smiling, I immediately think of Ned and how he suspected that Lady Eleanor had been with the king recently. "It is such a pleasure to meet you."

Gently pulling me closer, Eleanor whispers in my ear, "I believe that we are to travel to Warwick and then onto London together. I sincerely hope so, as I could do with a friend."

With these words, Eleanor looks sad, as if she is about to cry. Prior Michael, seeing the tears in Eleanor's huge eyes, directs her to a large chair next to me. Eva then smooths her kirtle and plumps the cushions about her, before retiring to sit next to Morris. I do hope that Morris behaves himself!

Once everyone is seated, two monks carry in a huge bowl of steaming hot apple juice and proceed to serve it. I can smell pepper, ginger and cardamom. The steam combined with the spices are making my nose tingle, and I attempt to sneeze as quietly as possible. Taking a linen kerchief from the pocket of my kirtle, I am distracted by what looks like a crumpled piece of parchment on the floor. I wonder what it could be. Looking around, I note that everyone is busy, either talking or being served, so I quickly stretch out my leg, cover the small piece of parchment with my foot and draw it close to me. Checking once more to make sure that I am unobserved, I drop my kerchief and retrieve the parchment. Placing it in my pocket, I decide to look at it when I retire for the night. If I'm not mistaken, I can feel that it was once sealed with wax, and a few broken bits of wax remain.

After the drink, the food is served. A feast of roast lamb, apple fritters and tansy cake. Rather than try the meat first, I decide to break a piece of tansy cake and let it melt in my mouth. The taste of tansy is pleasantly sweet, but strong at the same time. I say tansy cake, when, in reality, they are tansy fritters – made by combining the juice of the tansy plant with a plain batter, before being fried in butter until they are brown and crispy. At home, we used to call them 'golden suns', as this best describes the tansy flowers and the appearance of the cooked fritters. However, I refrain from eating more than a mouthful, as tansy flowers can be poisonous.

The roast lamb, although delicious, has been basted in what tastes like goose fat and rosemary, making it a little too greasy for my liking. However, the mint sauce that accompanies it is wonderful. Looking to my left, I notice that Eleanor is eating very little. Instead, she is pushing the food around her plate in an attempt to make it look like she's eating it. I also notice that Eleanor is scanning the floor, looking for something. I wonder if the piece of parchment in my pocket belongs to her, and if it does, what it says. How I wish the festivities were over.

Once everyone has eaten, the remnants of the meal are collected by numerous monks. I expect that they will be taken to the gatehouse and distributed as alms to the poor folk of Worksop. We are now to be entertained by a group of dancers known as morris dancers. One of their number enter the hall through the farthest door, sound a fanfare and call for silence. With our full attention now guaranteed, the solo fanfare player calls to the other eleven, who enter the hall in two lines. All of the men are dressed the same in dark hose and tunics. On their feet, they wear wooden clogs, and around their ankles, they have a band of small bells. Upon their heads, they wear holly wreaths. Each holds a solid staff in their right hand, which is decorated with ribbons of coloured fabric. They are a sight to behold. Once the fanfare player has exchanged his trumpet for his decorated staff, he gives a sign and the dancing commences.

First, they process around the hall at an even pace, bowing to people as they pass. Then, the tempo begins to speed up and they circle the hall, in the fashion of the sun rising and circling in the sky. Their feet stomp loudly on the floor and their ribbons swirl in the air, before they begin to prance manically and jump high into the air. I muse on the timing and the synchronisation of the dancers, as they move perfectly in time with one another. With not a footstep out of place, their clogs rise and fall in unison.

When the dancing stops, a solo musician begins to play and it's a musician that I know all too well. Ned, unable to control himself, has produced his shawm and is intent on joining in. Having found the morris dancers' spare ribbons and bells, he is now circling the hall wearing only his hose, ankle bells and a scarf tied loosely at his neck. The room descends into laughter as he leaps into the air before playing a merry tune. Far from being annoyed, the morris dancers also leap in the air and tap their clogs on the floor. If this evening's display is anything to go by, the slumbering spirits will have no option but to wake up and ensure a fertile spring, with a good harvest for all.

Next, and once the morris dancers have all retired to the side of the hall, the monks manoeuvre in a rickety wooden pageant wagon and, with the help of Prior Michael, who is playing the role of God, begin to enact the mystery play of Noah and the Arc. It's a play that depicts a flood so great that it threatens to wipe out all life on Earth. This destruction, however, is avoided by God who calls on the faithful Noah to build an arc and then to stock it with two of each species, thus ensuring that life is reborn and rebirth enabled. The stocking of the arc is very comical as two lambs, two piglets and two calves have all been released into the hall. With delight, they squeal as they run around, before the monks round them up and persuade them to climb the plank into the wagon. Once loaded, the arc is pushed from the hall, accompanied by the sound of loud clapping and cheering.

I sense that the festivities are drawing to a close and I suspect that the hall is being cleared for the final activity of Pace Egging. Pace Egging, in this instance, consists of rolling finely decorated eggs in a straight line through a set of arches and wickets. The winner is the person who rolls the egg in the straightest line possible and through all of the obstacles. As usual, Ned has assumed the top role and is carrying the large glass bowl with the eggs into the hall. He places it with care in between me and Eleanor on the top table and retreats with a naughty grin on his face. Eleanor smiles weakly and looks concerned. I wonder if she still seeks the small piece of parchment that lies within my pocket. The trumpet sounds once more and the surveyor of the hall enters through a small and largely concealed door to my right. Immediately, I recognise the shape of the hooded and cloaked man. He is tall and straight and holds himself with a sense of purpose. As he approaches, I begin to shake violently and I struggle to contain my emotions. I must not smile and betray the identity of the surveyor. A strong smell of mint circles in the air as he leans in close to me. Only his eyes are visible. Eyes that I know and love with all my heart. Pip is here with me!

Back in my room, with Peter keeping a lookout outside, I pace up and down and think of Pip. I wonder how long he has been with us, if I will see him again, and if the others know of his presence. How I long to be in his arms, to feel his muscular body holding me safe, to kiss his soft lips and stroke his hair. Suddenly, I see a shadow cross the room and hear quiet footsteps approach from behind the heavy tapestry hanging. I hold my breath and prepare to scream. For the shadow could be that of Pip, but it could equally be an enemy. To my dismay, it is the latter and I scream for help and run to the door.

Within seconds, Peter is by my side. However, the shadow person is far too quick and nimble for Peter on this occasion, and whoever it is escapes. Not wanting to leave me alone, Peter closes the door.

"Mistress Bethany, I am so sorry. I had no choice but to remain by your side, even if that meant that the shadow person escaped. I could not risk you being attacked."

Gratefully, I let Peter guide me towards the bed, where I sit down and catch my breathe. As I do, Peter ransacks the room and checks for any hidden entry points.

"I just can't work out how that shadow person entered this room. I checked everywhere thoroughly myself before you returned, and I never left the door, not even for one second."

Then, with all his might, Peter tugs at the heavy tapestry hanging. Surprisingly, it remains in place and reveals nothing. Moving on, Peter asks me to move to the stool in the corner of the room before he pushes the bed to one side.

"Ah-ha… what do we have here?!"

I am shocked to see a hidden trapdoor within the floorboards.

"Now, this explains all. It would seem that this trapdoor allows entry into the room, but once in, there is no exit apart from the door. Whoever that was managed to manoeuvre their way in but became trapped. They cannot have been a member of the community, as I'm sure that they would know how these type of trapdoors work. The person must have been an outsider looking for something."

Instantly, I remember the small piece of parchment in my pocket and turn to Peter. "Perhaps they were looking for this." I stand and walk over to the bed, before carefully removing the parchment and laying it down. As I unwrap it, tiny pieces of red wax are scattered all around.

Peter, moving closer, looks at the remainer of the seal. "I know this device; it is that of the Butler family. This must belong to Lady Eleanor Talbot. Where did you find this, Mistress?"

"I found it in the great hall by the top table, just after Lady Eleanor took her seat. Feeling inquisitive, I covered it with my foot, drew it close and concealed it within my pocket when no one was looking."

"Did Lady Eleanor say anything about losing something?"

"Oh no, she just kept looking around and her demeanour certainly changed."

"No wonder, what this says is deadly." I look in horror at the piece of parchment. "Mistress, this is part of an order, which clearly mentions kidnap. How I wish that there was more of this document. The only words that I can clearly distinguish speak of the Butler lands being exchanged for the king's brothers, Richard and George."

"Peter, we must summon Ned and Alard at once."

"Yes, but I cannot leave you and you cannot go alone. Fetch your cloak and we'll go in search of the others."

By good fortune, we find everyone huddled together in the stables. How strange. I wonder what they were all doing. On entering, they look up, obviously startled to see us. Even Liege and Freemantle raise their heads, before lying down again.

Alard stands. "Peter, Mistress Bethany, what are you doing? Peter, you should be guarding Mistress Bethany in her room."

Sitting, we recount the events in my room.

Ned is the first to speak. "So, what we thought to be true is actually the case. There is a plan afoot to kidnap the king's brothers and to kill the king after his coronation. We must act decisively and we must not arouse any suspicions. We are heavily outnumbered by Lady Eleanor's retainers, so there is only one thing for it. Rather than forcibly retain Lady Eleanor, she must be wooed, and we have the right person here to do it. Owain, you are from a landed family and could be considered a good catch."

To this, we all laugh, as Owain rolls his eyes.

"You must seek out Lady Eleanor and enchant her. Use your wit and charm by all means, but do not touch her, not even one kiss. She must be smitten by you and your attention. She is well known for being vain, so shower her with compliments and acts of courtly love. Then, Davy, you must do the same with Eva de Mortain. You are both of equal status and it will not seem strange. Follow her everywhere and keep a close eye on her. Even without seeing the shadow person, I would bet that it was her. Who else would be small enough to climb through the trapdoor and hide beneath the bed, before concealing themselves behind the tapestry? Not a man, that's for sure."

To this, Davy and Owain both nod in agreement.

"Peter, please take Mistress Bethany back to her room. We must act as normal as possible in every way. If you are seen, explain that Mistress Bethany has a sore head and that you thought that the fresh night air might help. Tomorrow, we will travel with Lady Eleanor's baggage train. I doubt that any of her retainers are involved in this as plots like this only work if they are kept a secret, and it's more than likely that the Butler family are blackmailing Eleanor without anyone apart from her maid knowing. We are safe enough."

Before we leave, I turn and ask, "How strange that you were all here together. Have you been dicing, or have you had a visitor?"

To this, everyone smiles, with Alard noting, "Yes, an old friend passed by. He also travels to Warwick. I'm sure that we'll catch-up with him again at some point."

Smiling, I realise that they have also seen Pip and, in his stealthy manner, he is directing operations from a distance. With a sense of peace in my heart, I bid goodnight and let Peter guide me back to my room. Luckily, we pass no one and we do not have to explain our travels. After Peter has checked my room, I fall into a deep, dreamless, heavy sleep.

The morning breaks with strong sunshine glistening on the snow. The sky is clear blue and a chill hangs on the air. After breaking our fast in the hall together, we are ready to take our place in Lady Eleanor's baggage train. Morris, having prepared Liege and Freemantle, brings the cart around to the hall doorway and I climb aboard, after thanking Prior Michael for both his hospitality and the Easter festivities.

"Thank you so much, Prior Michael, I have never celebrated Easter in such style. It's such a shame that my husband could not have been here with us."

To this, Prior Michael gives a wry smile and I realise that he must also have seen Pip. With a wave goodbye, the baggage train begins to move slowly away – *slowly* being the optimum word. At least today's journey will not put a strain on either Liege or Freemantle. If anything, they look rather happy to be plodding along at walking pace. I also feel happy, for although there is a deadly plot afoot, we have the culprit in our sights and those who engage with her will also be in our sights. Therefore, I sit back and enjoy the journey.

The Caves of Nottingham Castle

On our way to Nottingham Castle, we travel through Sherwood Forest. An ancient royal forest so vast that I struggle to comprehend its size. Morris says that Sherwood Forest stretches nearly all the way from Worksop Castle to Nottingham Castle, with adult stags and heavily pregnant does roaming free.

"See over there, Mistress – those older stags with the fearsome antlers. They rule the roost, while, over there, the younger ones wait for their turn to be in charge. We'll be safe enough, as long as we leave them alone. They're used to travellers passing through. In the time of my great-grandfather, there used to be a large palace near here, which was visited by all the Plantagenet kings from King Henry II to King Richard II." We cross ourselves at the latter's name. "Although, nowadays, the Palace of Kings lies in ruins, and the stone is robbed out to build homesteads in the nearby hamlets and villages. Rabbit warrens now take its place, and the area grows ever wealthier each year – but with wealth comes other problems. Robbers and gangs are said to lurk in the coppices and seek out targets. Have you heard of the Ballad of Robin Hood, Bethany?"

"No, Morris, what is the ballad about?"

"Well, it's long been thought that there is a man called Robin Hood who lives in the forest, who steals from the rich and gives to the poor. Some say that he's a member of the aristocracy with a hatred towards the local sheriff, while others say that he has a deeply held devotion to the Virgin Mary and a great respect for women. No one really knows. Others say that they have seen him and that he is clad from head to toe in green with a jaunty cap. It's most probably a myth, as the name Robin Hood is a well-known alias, but it's always good to have a local story to tell travellers. Robin is supposed to roam the forest with his band of supporters including Friar Tuck and Maid Marian. The legend of Robin Hood is travelling at an alarming speed round the country, and, in some parts, there are even May Day games being dedicated to him."

I wonder quietly to myself if that's the reasoning behind Owain's choice of attire, for he is wearing head to toe green and is walking alongside Lady Eleanor's cart. Perhaps he is trying to lure her into thinking that she is his Maid Marian. Even from this distance, I can hear Owain singing love ballads to her. I just wish that I could see her face and not the back of her head. It's terribly frustrating.

As we travel further through the forest, I can see areas of snow being cleared and saplings being planted. Although this seems strange at first, I remember being told that the snow can insulate the ground and protect young plants. The saplings will ensure that the forest is reborn and that the animals that live within it will be provided for. Looking to my left, there are huge piles of felled trees everywhere – certainly, for as far as the eye can see. I expect that they are being left to age. On my right-hand side, men are using small hand axes to remove the bark from the trees. No doubt once this is done, the wood will be transported all over the country, as aged wood is always in high demand for building. Further on, there is a large pond.

"See over there, Mistress – that pond was once known as Clipsham Peel. I have no idea why, but I do know that it supplied all the fish to the Palace of Kings. Nowadays, only the locals fish there." Morris goes silent for a moment and I can see from his eyes that he is remembering his youth. "I used to love fishing when I was young, but the water wouldn't suit my old bones nowadays."

This gets me thinking about my times past and especially my time at the priory at Castle Acre, where the monks both fish and wash in the fast-flowing stream that meanders its way through the priory grounds.

Morris wakes me from my revere. "The Earls of March have historically owned this land and, in particular, the Mortimers, who are looked on as friends in this area, but I'll tell you more about that when we get to Nottingham Castle."

By the time we reach the outskirts of Nottingham, the sky has become grey and overcast, and the snow has started to fall once more. Heavy clouds darken the sky and an intense fear washes over me. In the distance, I can see the sandstone castle, sitting high upon the ridge. The only thing separating us is the mighty River Trent. Looking up, I can see King Edward's standard flying magnifically from the top tower of the castle. Pride wells up inside of me, for this castle is where

King Edward chose to proclaim himself the rightful King of England before travelling to Towton to secure his claim and put down his enemies. I contemplate the events that led Edward to this decision and the symbolism of announcing his claim at Nottingham Castle.

Once over the river, we enter the castle through the outer bailey. This is where the baggage train separates, with only our cart and Lady Eleanor's travelling into the inner bailey. Feeling an immense sense of calm, I am reassured by the vast number of retainers wearing the king's livery. I had heard that King Edward had ordered that the castle be turned into a fortress, but, in reality, I didn't really know what a fortress would look like.

On our arrival, we are met by a large man in bright-red velvet robes and a green velvet cap. To my surprise, he heads in our direction first, rather than in Lady Eleanor's.

"Welcome, Lady Harsyck, we have been expecting you. Please let me introduce myself – I am Sir William Herbert, the first Lord of Pembroke, and the first full-blooded Welshman to enter the English Peerage." With this, Sir William puffs out his chest, before bowing low. "Our dearest king, King Eward IV, requested that I leave my native land of Wales and oversee the strengthening and rebuilding of this castle. Your arrival coincides with the digging of a new and extremely deep dry ditch. A waterless moat, which is just as effective as a water-filled one. Come, let me show you."

Taking Sir William's hand, I climb down from the cart and follow him to the outer bailey. As I pass Lady Eleanor's cart, I can't help but notice the look of anger on her face and I presume that she is annoyed at not being greeted first. Continuing to avoid her direct gaze, I look into the distance and consider the way that Lady Eleanor seeks special attention from all. However, I think that she will soon regain her look of innocence and air of grandeur as a far younger man – who I presume is related to Sir William – is welcoming her to the castle. Hopefully, his attention will allow poor Owain to rest. For when he was chosen to woo her, no one could have known how demanding she would be.

Looking down into the deep dry ditch, the first thing that hits me is the variation in the colour of the soil. Completely unlike the Fens, this soil is made from various shade of red. I have heard that Shrewsbury Castle appears almost pink due to its construction from red sandstone, and now I can understand how that could happen. Returning to the inner baily, I look around and watch as the encampment grows ever larger and canopies are erected.

Sir William is the first to speak. "Have no fear, Lady Harsyck. Your retainers will be lodged in the castle with you. They will not have to rest here." I gratefully nod my head, as I should have hated them to be so far from me. "Your horses will also be lodged within the stables of the inner bailey."

After thanking Sir William, we continue to walk in the direction of the main tower of the castle. Sir William has the look of an old comrade who seen many battles but is now wrapped in the life of luxury. His hair is as white as the gently falling snow.

Stopping abruptly once inside the calm of the inner bailey, Sir William turns to face me. "Lady Harsyck, I want you to rest assured in the knowledge that I am aware of the kidnap plot and the involvement of Lady Eleanor – that is why my eldest son has welcomed her, instead of myself. Daffyd will keep an eye on her and my other son, Allen, will keep a watch on her maid, Eva. They will not be able to move a foot without being watched, and with all their retainers lodged in the outer bailey, they will be isolated and unable to make any trouble."

Surprised and taken aback by the frankness of Sir William, I struggle to find the right words. How on earth did he know about the kidnap plot? Seeming to read my thoughts, Sir William takes my hand and explains that he was and will always be a loyal supporter of the House of York and King Edward – in exactly the same way that he was completely loyal to Richard, Duke of York right up until his death a few months ago. Looking deep into Sir William's eyes, I can see the tears of pain that bubble just beneath the surface and realise that I have no reason to fear my stay at Nottingham Castle.

Inside, I am happily reunited with Ned, who explains that the others are busy unpacking our trunks and preparing our accommodation on the south side of the castle.

"You'll love your room, Bethany; it has the largest solar window seat that I've ever seen, and I'm told that the views are spectacular. You are lodged in the late Queen Isabella's apartment. I have been told that the furnishings have been updated over the years, but in essence the solar has remained true to Queen Isabella's vision."

On hearing this, my heart jumps for joy. I then contemplate Queen Isabella and Roger Mortimer's great love and passion for each other – something that I could never have understood before my marriage to Pip. How they were not only devoted to each other, but how they were driven to do the right thing for the country, even in the face of major opposition. Their fight against King Edward II and his corrupt ways, the Despenser family and their malign influence over the king, and the way that the Mortimer inheritance was vehemently dismissed, must have been draining.

Ned coughs lightly, as a way to regain my attention.

"Oh, Ned, I'm so sorry. I was just thinking about Roger Mortimer and Queen Isabella."

To this, Ned laughs. "I gathered that. Come on, let's go inside. The snow fall is getting heavier."

Inside, we head straight for the hall. The solar will have to wait for a while. I want to observe Lady Eleanor and Eva.

The great hall certainly lives up to its name. It is a riot of gold, white and green. Looking up, I immediately notice that finely decorated lamps are hanging from elaborate wall sconces, their candles burning brightly, and their light being diffused through a variety of glass panels within the lamps. The dais is adorned with a mass of ivy and golden ribbons. It would seem that no expense has been spared, as all of the tables are also decorated with golden lamps, golden ribbon and ivy drapes.

I look around for Lady Eleanor and Eva and find them sitting deep in conversation upon the dais. Upon seeing me, Eva immediately stands and vacates the dais to sit on a side table. Both look at me with ill-concealed hatred, which I take no notice of. I welcome them both as friends and ask if they had a good journey. Lady Eleanor is the only one to speak.

"No, we did not enjoy our journey. One of your retinue would simply not leave me alone. I believe his name to be Owain. He certainly fancies himself, that's for sure. If he wasn't singing to me, he was reciting poetry or speaking about his great passion of juggling. He even asked me to meet him before we retire, so that he could show me his balls. Well, as if someone in my position would ever fall for such a low-grade buffoon. I certainly have no interest in his juggling balls and my maid, Eva, certainly has no interest in Davy from your retinue either. Please could I ask you to keep them in check."

Choking, I feign that I cannot breathe, but this is simply a ruse to cover up my desire to burst out laughing. Owain and Davy have performed their duties perfectly. Lady Eleanor makes her excuses and leaves with Eva.

While they are absent, Ned kneels before me and speaks quietly, "Bethany, I have just received a message from King Edward. He is extremely grateful that you have procured evidence of the kidnap plot. Alas, he is also sad to learn that Lady Eleanor is one of the perpetrators, though he would rather know the truth."

I nod and feel sad for the king, as betrayal is always hard to take.

Ned continues, "King Edward has had the piece of parchment checked against the handwriting of Lady Eleanor among others, and his scouts have confirmed that Lady Eleanor; her maid, Eva de Mortain; Thomas Stanley, Earl of Derby; and Ralph Boteler, Lord Sudeley were all seen together at Towton, just a day before the battle. We had all wondered why she was in the vicinity of Towton Hall so soon after the battle, but we had just presumed that King Edward had secretly summoned her. We were all wrong; it was Lady Eleanor who had sought out King Edward and then pretended to comfort him. When asked, King Edward mentioned a possible precontract of marriage to Lady Eleanor, but he wouldn't elaborate on the details. So, we may never know whether there was a ceremony or not, but we do know that Lady Eleanor and Eva may have been dabbling in magic to try to secure Eleanor's place as Queen of England. On inspection of their belongings, numerous small bottles of potions and sage sticks have been found, along with books of spells and items related to astrology."

I immediately cross myself. "So, you're saying that they're both witches?"

"No, not witches, but certainly deluded and foolish individuals."

I consider their fate before speaking, "Ned, what happens next?"

"Well, it's all very tricky. We can't risk the other plotters knowing that the kidnap plot has been uncovered, so both Eleanor and Eva have been arrested and charged with witchcraft. Their retainers will be advised of this in the morning and the baggage train will leave without them. We doubt that their families will rise up against the king, so we should be able to hold them until the plot has been foiled, and then, if there is enough evidence, they will both be charged along with aspiring to kidnap."

Thinking of the dungeons makes me shiver. "Will they be housed respectfully in the dungeons?"

"Of course. They will share a clean cell with a bed and a privy. Completely isolated, they will be well fed and treated respectfully. The only person that they will see will be Sir William Herbert, lest they try to tempt a guard to convey messages for them to the outside world."

"Ned, Morris mentioned that the Mortimers are looked on kindly by the folk of this area, but I'm certain that Roger Mortimer was trapped and taken from Nottingham Castle to his death. Is that correct?"

"Ah yes, that's true, but I haven't enough time to tell you of that at the moment, as I can see that the servers are getting restless, and we don't want to ruin the meal, do we? So, I'll retire to my seat for now, but afterwards I'll return with a surprise."

With that, Ned smiles and heads towards the others.

The meal passes me by in a daze, as I speculate on what the surprise could be. Even the delicious taste of fresh eggs baked in a salt crust with nettle bread cannot drag my thoughts away from the surprise.

Sir William Herbert proves to be a most attentive host and, noticing that I am in a dream world, pulls his chair closer. "Lady Harsyck, are you well? Does the food not please you?"

Realising that I have been remiss, I smile. "Oh, please forgive me, I have been lost in my thoughts. The food is absolutely delicious."

At this, Sir William turns his head away from the room and speaks to me. "Lady Harsyck – please may I call you Lady Bethany? As we share the same allegiances, it would be nice to be slightly less formal." Without the need to think, I readily agree. "Thank you, Lady Bethany, and now that the meal is being cleared away, would you allow me to summon Ned and Alard to accompany us to my inner chamber?"

Nodding, I gratefully agree.

Sir William's chamber is a brightly coloured fusion of red, green and gold from floor to ceiling, with a black chevron design running around the middle of the room. A fine tapestry depicting a fire-breathing dragon hangs upon the furthest wall. More lamps light the room and a fire burns within the modern fireplace, which is located against the outer wall. Amazingly, the smoke is drawn up the chimney and away from the room. Five chairs have been positioned in the middle of the room around a round table. I wonder who the fifth person will be. Perhaps Daffyd or Allen?

We take our seats and are served wine and cheese by a very elderly man. The wine tastes smooth and spicy, and the cheese is soft and creamy. What a lovely way to end the day. Warm and sated. I relax and listen as Sir William, Ned and Alard talk about the building work that is due to begin. It would seem that King Edward has magnificent plans for Nottingham Castle.

After what seems an age, there's a soft knock upon the door.

"Ah-ha, our visitor has arrived." Sir William calls to the guard to open the door and it slowly opens.

To my delight, Charlemain is standing in the doorway. I immediately rise to my feet and run to him. Embracing him, I begin to sob happy tears. The room is alight with joy. "Oh, Charlemain, what a wonderful surprise. I have missed you. Are you well? Is Dowager Lady Harsyck well? Is Roger well? Will you be travelling with us? I have so many questions."

A beaming Charlemain takes my arm and we are soon seated. "Dearest Bethany, we are all very well and South Acre is as beautiful as ever. How we all miss you and Pip being there."

"It's good to see you, Charlemain," says Sir William. "I knew that you would soon give up the luxury of South Acre and return to travelling."

"Yes, the time has come for me to accompany Bethany. Warwick Castle is a viper's nest at the best of times, and I must be there to protect and assist Bethany in any way that I can."

To this, everyone nods. Alard rises and walks to the fireplace. I can sense that he has something to say. Shuffling from one foot to the other, he prepares to speak, "Well, there's never a good time to speak about such things, but they must be spoken of. Now that Lady Eleanor and her maid are incarcerated and guarded in the dungeons below, we must move swiftly. At first light, whatever the weather, we must leave for Leicester. Owain, Davy and Morris are preparing for our departure as we speak. Bethany, from now on, I'm afraid that you will have to travel in the back of the cart, as Davy will ride next to Morris. Davy has a very keen eye and will be an excellent lookout. Ned and I will walk either side of the cart, and Peter will walk behind. I doubt that there is any imminent danger, but Thomas Stanley and Ralph Boteler will surely wonder where Lady Eleanor and her maid are – although, in reality, I doubt that they would be foolish enough to ask. Anyway, I suspect that it would suit Lord Sudeley if Lady Eleanor was to vanish, and as for Thomas Stanley, he won't care in the slightest. She is nothing to him, just a pawn to be used to further his ambitions, but we must be careful none the less."

After a few minutes, I break the thoughtful silence of the room. "Sir William, if you permit, I would like to see the caves and tunnels of this castle before I leave. I understand that Roger Mortimer was captured and trapped here, and that he was forcibly torn from Queen Isabella's arms. As Roger Mortimer is a distant relative, I feel the need to see the place where he was taken."

A nodding Sir William agrees, and Morris is called for.

As we carefully navigate the steep stone steps, we both take extreme care to hold onto the rope, which is attached to the wall via a collection of small metal loops. "Now, Mistress Bethany, please let me lead the way, as I have a little knowledge of these caves."

"Morris, have you been here before then?"

"Oh yes, many years ago, when I was a lad. I used to visit Nottingham Castle with my father. I never really knew why; he just used to tell me to mind my own business and not to ask any questions, as what you didn't know couldn't hurt you. So, I learnt not to ask." Morris chuckles. "Fortunately, the stone is not too slippery today. I've been here when there's been running water gushing all over the place, but they seem to have solved that problem. They've also fitted wall sconces since my last visit and the light is really quite good now."

In my mind, I try to imagine the caves as they must have been in Roger and Isabella's times. Cold, damp and extremely dark. I then shiver at the very thought. Once at the bottom of the stairs, I ask about the tunnels. "Morris, how on earth do you escape from here? The tunnels seem never-ending."

"That's how they're supposed to appear, but if you come with me, this smaller tunnel leads to fields beyond the outer bailey. In the daytime, you can see a small chink of light at the very end; apart from that, you need to know which one to follow. Roger Mortimer would have known exactly how to escape and where to meet his followers. Alas, he never made it this far, as he was cruelly bound and gagged, before being taken to the Tower of London, where he was condemned without standing trial – but, Mistress, please do not distress yourself with the details. What's done is done, and you need to preserve all your energy for the task in hand. By your investigations, you will be able to save lives."

As we turn and begin to climb the stairs, I hear a high-pitched woman's voice call out, "Fair son, have pity on me and gentle Mortimer."

I look around, but I'm unable to see anyone. "Morris, did you hear that?"

"Hear what, Mistress?"

"A woman's voice calling out."

"Sorry, Mistress, I heard nothing, but I expect that you heard Queen Isabella calling to her son, King Edward III. It's been said that Queen Isabella's ghost has been seen pacing up and down the tunnels over the years. She searches for Mortimer and implores that her son spares Mortimer. Her words are said to be trapped within the stone."

Without Morris noticing, I kiss my hand and then press it hard against the stone, trying desperately to impart my love into the stones, and both Isabella and Mortimer's hearts.

Upstairs in the comfort of the solar, with both Alard and Peter lodged close by, I remove my shoes, outer clothes and coif. How I long to bathe in hot water, but as there is no barrel to sit and soak in, I make do with a bowl of cold water and a linen towel. I do not have the energy to call for water at this late hour, so I wash quickly before climbing into bed. After saying my prayers, I settle down to sleep.

However, I am forced to sit up when I feel an icy blast of cold air wash over me. I scour the room for intruders, but there are none, only a disappearing white mist and a small blue sapphire, which has appeared next to my wooden cross. I wonder how on earth it got there. I pick it up and roll it around in my hand. It is smooth and, on closer inspection, I notice that it is set within a golden clasp. Turning it over, there is a tiny oval link attached, which I presume allows it to be worn upon a chain. How strange for it to simply appear out of nowhere. It certainly could not have rolled into that position.

Then, all of a sudden, I understand. The white mist was Isabella's spirit and the sapphire must have been carved from the Mortimer sapphire, which I unknowingly carried to Walsingham. The same sapphire that foretold my future and confirmed my lineage. Queen Isabella has given this to me for protection. My heart swells with emotion as I quietly speak Isabella's name. Climbing from my bed, I go over to my chest, which sits by the window seat. Ned was right – this is the largest solar seat that I have ever seen. In fact, it's so large that I'm certain that I could lie down upon the single cushion and sleep here all night.

Opening my chest, I use the moonlight to guide me to a velvet small pouch. Unfortunately, I do not own a chain, but I do have a fine set of silk points, which were woven for me at South Acre. They were a wedding present from my mother-in-law. I just hope that the fine tip at the end will thread through the oval link. To my surprise, when I push the tip, it glides through the link with ease and, to my delight, remains in place and does not fall off, even when I shake it and gently tug at it. *Excellent.* I will now be able to wear the sapphire as either a necklace or a bracelet on very special occasions, but for now I tie it securely into the hem of my cloak. Feeling a sense of peace, I lie upon the cushion and cover myself with my cloak. As I drift off to sleep in the solar window, I can't help but long for the morning!

I awake to find myself bathed in glorious sunshine. The day has broken and the view is magnificent. Birds circle in the sky and the white snow blankets everything in its wake. The branches hang heavy with icicles and the newly spun spider's webs glisten.

Before long, there is a knock at the door and I hear Ned call out to me, "Bethany, are you awake? We need to leave shortly."

"Yes, Ned, I'm awake. Please just give me a few moments more to prepare myself and I'll be with you." When dressed and ready to go, I allow myself just one look back towards the solar seat before I unlock the door and leave.

The road to Leicester is completely straight and packed with travellers even at this early hour. Sir William, having concerns for our safety, has provided us with a group of retainers and we are to be joined along the way by others loyal to Duke Richard and his family. In essence, we now have our own baggage train, and I appear as a fine lady being escorted across the country. This image will be extremely advantageous and will allow me to blend in seamlessly when we arrive at Warwick Castle. Dressed in my old brown woollen kirtle and matching coif, I sit next to Charlemain on a cushioned wooden seat.

"Bethany, this is just like old times, but much better. How my feet used to ache after walking from village to village. A cart ride is much better, especially when my dear old friend Morris is in charge."

To this, Morris begins to laugh. "If only I was in charge – Liege is pulling so hard this morning that Fremantle, Davy and myself are as much passengers as you are. We're letting him lead the way, safe in the knowledge that he can't go wrong. He must follow the straight road all the way to Burton on the Wolds, where we will stop to break our fast."

As planned, Ned, Alard and Peter walk either side and behind the cart – but where's Owain? I look around and search for him without any luck.

Calling to Alard, I am concerned. "Alard, where is Owain? Is he safe? I can't see him – is he with us?"

A laughing Alard replies, "Do not fear! Owain will rejoin us at Burton. He has stayed behind to serenade Lady Eleanor and Eva. He thought that it would be a pleasant wake-up call."

To this, we all laugh and relax into the day.

True to Alard's word, Owain rejoins us at Burton on the Wolds and with him he has bought a vast selection of delights, some of which are still warm. While stationary, and located in a clearing by a large stone way-marker, we turn the cart into a dining area. Alard is laying out wooden trenchers and cups, while Ned unpacks the food and Owain pours the refreshments. To everyone's delight, there is more than plenty of bacon, sausages, cheese and fried bread for everyone. While Morris is treating Liege and Fremantle to a bundle of hay, I notice that we have been joined by a new horse. It is black with a sleek coat. It has a finely platted mane and tail, with golden ribbons woven into both. It is dressed in studded leather armour, which is emblazoned with the coat of arms of Sir William. This, no doubt, is how Owain caught up with us so quickly. While everything is being cleared away, I seek out Owain.

"My, oh my, what a fine steed, Owain. What's his name?"

With a huge smile on his face, Owain loosens the horse's leather straps and brings him closer to me, rubbing his nose and ears all the time. "His name is Lightning and he's a gentle old soul. Steady but speedy at the same time. Alas, he is merely on loan to me. Sir William thought that he needed some exercise and I was glad to oblige. He'll be heading back to Nottingham very soon, with one of Sir William's men. How I wish that he were mine."

Once Lightning has been reclaimed by Sir William's messenger, we are on our way once more. I now have two fine gentleman to point things out to me. Morris, having a far greater knowledge of the area, proceeds to tell me about the four windmills that we passed on our way out of Nottingham.

"Those windmills have been used by travellers ever since the reign of King Henry IV, way before the Battle of Agincourt, as way-markers and stopping points. Not only does each windmill have its own miller, but it also has its own alewife, too. All of the windmills have names. There's Sparrow, Donne, Dosse and Gloff. Daft names, if you ask me, but they no doubt meant something to the person who named them."

As we approach Leicester, we slow down to almost a walking pace. Morris then explains that Leicester is a complete nightmare of a place.

"First, you have to cross the River Soar or its tributaries, and then you have to navigate the Roman walls and the gateways, which are so small that some of the newer carts just can't get through them. We'll be alright, though, as I'm old-fashioned and I know what works, but the cart drivers that can't enter will either have to back up or turn around completely. Then their inhabitants will have to dismount and walk to their destinations, carrying all their luggage with them. This causes much chaos and a great deal of delay. I know that I shouldn't, but I have often waved at stranded people on my way past." Morris throws his head back and laughs wholeheartedly.

Both Charlemain and I try to suppress our smiles, but with little success.

Once inside the walls, we find ourself faced by a maze of roads, which all look exactly the same. Morris explains that all Roman towns are just the same.

"When the Romans invaded, they took over certain strategic locations all over the country and then they set about redesigning them. One of their first actions was always to realign the old roads and build new ones, and for this they used a well-developed grid system. The Romans were sticklers for organisation and rule. The layout may look confusing, but in reality you can never really get lost, as you'll just go round and round in circles within the walls."

Morris then starts describing where we will be staying. "We'll be staying at the Greyfriars. More formally known as the Order of the Friars Minor. As you both know, Richard, Duke of York held close ties with the Friars Minors at Leicester and elsewhere, and they are our friends. Thus, King Edward has bestowed a great deal of honours on the Franciscans in Leicester, as a way of saying thank you for their loyalty to the House of York. Inside their chapel, which is dedicated to St Francis and St Mary Magdalen, I hear that they have a specially commissioned lifelike wooden effigy of Richard, Duke of York, surrounded by hundreds of candles and beeswax tapers. They say prayers for his soul and his family, both day and night."

Feeling a little unsettled, I both long to see the effigy and to offer up my prayers, but I'm also scared of what I'll see. The horrors of seeing Duke Richard's cold and lifeless body lying in rest at Pontefract Castle still haunts me. Charlemain, obviously noting the horror on my face, asks Morris to explain a little more about the route to the Greyfriars.

Happy to explain, Morris continues, "Greyfriars is located on the opposite side of the town and the friary covers a very large area. We'll be approaching via St Francis's Lane from the north, but the friary is equally accessible from the south, via Friar Lane. The whole complex is enclosed, behind a very sturdy brick wall, with both the north and south entrances having solid oak gates, which are reinforced with hammered metalwork. Inside Greyfriars, the precinct wraps itself around the central buildings, the cloisters and the chapel. The Friars Minor are almost entirely self-sufficient, you see. I would liken the friary to a small village set within a town."

As we travel through the narrow streets, I see a variety of names, most of which I have never encountered before. The names that stick out most are Loseby Lane, Cank Street, Gallowtree Gate, Sanvey Gate and Holy Bones.

"Morris, do you know the meanings of the various street names in this area?"

"Of course, Mistress – you should know by now that I know everything there is to know about everything."

To this, both Charlemain and I laugh out loud before Charlemain comments, "Really? that's not what Alice says."

"Ha! What does that old bat know about anything?"

Content to have wound Morris up, Charlemain makes amends by agreeing that Alice is, indeed, old. The others also laugh and Ned calls out, "Well, Morris, you may not rate Alice very highly, but you certainly like her red-haired beauty of a daughter, Honey Morton."

Morris concedes and joins in with the laughter. "Yes, you're right there, Ned."

To spare Morris any further blushes, I ask him to explain the street names. "They're quite easy really. Loseby Lane is named after Henry de Loseby, a local landowner. Loseby Lane is where the cattle market meets twice a week. Cank Street is named after the local well. Sanvey Gate leads to the Sancta Via, otherwise known as the Holy Way, where religious processions wend their way to St Margaret's Church. Holy Bones is the street between the butcher's shops and St Nicholas Church. Then, lastly, there is Gallowtree Gate. A dark place that leads out of town towards the gallows on the London Road."

The thought of the gallows terrifies me, as I remember being told that after Roger Mortimer was cruelly condemned to death without a trial, he was imprisoned within the Tower of London, before being dragged through the streets of London, wearing just a pair of torn plain hose and an old black tunic that he had worn when attending the funeral ceremony of King Edward II, Queen Isabella's false and unholy husband. His feet bloody and his ankles bound tightly. Then, after being allowed to give a short speech, he was dragged to the gallows, stripped naked and hung in the manner of a common criminal. His body was left to hang for days in full view. The indignity of his death, coupled with my distant connection, is just too much to bear. Unable to stop myself, my face becomes wet. Turning away from Charlemain, I dab my eyes dry and make a silent pledge to myself to visit Castle Rising when I return home to South Acre. Castle Rising being the castle where Queen Isabella was imprisoned by her very own son, King Edward III.

Refusing to focus on death and destruction, I look around at the beautiful buildings on either side of the high street. We pass a magnificent timbered inn named The White Boar. How splendid! I believe the white boar to be an ancient emblem used by the House of York. Further in the distance, the castle complex sits sorrily, high above the rooftops and the River Soar. Its turrets are blackened from a recent fire and its roof is almost entirely gone. As we turn a sharp right, Morris snorts and mentions the castle.

"I expect that the fire was caused by God's displeasure with the House of Lancaster, as the castle was once the favoured residence of both John of Gaunt and Henry Bolingbroke, the Duke of Lancaster. Word has it that King Edward has ordered that the Guilds of Leicester either repair it and rebuild it, or that they raise it to the ground. It's only fair, you see – the guilds grew rich from supporting the Crown; now, they can pay the Crown back."

I cross myself and feel extremely grateful that we are not residing at the castle, as its visage chills me to the bone.

Jolting to a halt, we stop in front of a pair of heavy oak gates, before Morris calls out, "We are here to see the successor of Friar John Holcote. My name is Morris and I have the honour of leading the baggage train of Lady Bethany Harsyck."

To this, a small side gate opens and a very young friar emerges. Charlemain then explains, "The friars here are naturally cautious, for in 1402, eight of their number and the master of divinity were arrested for supporting King Richard II. Those that were arrested were taken to London and stood before two separate juries, before being convicted by a third. In total, twelve of their number were executed."

We both cross ourselves. After satisfying the young friar of our identity, the young friar calls out that the gates can be opened. Inside, we are met by a small group of friars and a very tall man, who I presume to be Friar John Holcote's successor.

"Welcome, welcome, we have been expecting you. Alas, your private messenger has just left. Please let me introduce myself. My name is Friar John Hall."

Taking Friar John's hand, I climb down from the back of the cart and, once joined by Charlemain, follow the delegation of friars into the great hall. On our way, I lean over to Charlemain and whisper, "Do we have our own private messenger?"

"Oh yes, but we'll speak of that later." Charlemain smiles and continues to walk on.

The great hall, true to the rule of St Francis of Assisi, is actually very austere. Wooden tables and bench seats line the walls, while in the middle of the room is a very large hearth with a fire that burns and crackles. In the fire, I can count four large cauldrons. All of which have steam rising from them. The smell is absolutely delicious. In the farthest corner, there is a portable bread oven on wheels.

Friar John, noticing my interest, turns to me and speaks, "Please forgive the austerity of our house, but we adhere to the very strictest of rules. Not only do we grow nearly all our own food, but our friars beg for food as they preach. This food is then added to our supplies and cooked each evening, here in the hall. Then, after taking a ladle of vegetable pottage each and a piece of bread, we deliver the rest of the pottage and bread to both the north and south gates. This is then shared out among those who wait. However, I do not expect you or your retainers to go without. You have many miles to travel and you must keep your strength up, so I have instructed that the friars boil a large joint of bacon for you all to share."

Touched by such kindness, I reply, "Thank you so much, Friar John, that is most kind of you. However, if you would allow, I would like us all to share the bacon. Perhaps the joint could be cut into four and divided between all four cauldrons."

A smiling, Friar John nods in agreement and sends word to those who are cooking. "Please, come and sit with me, while your retainers prepare your room for the night."

Sitting to the side of the hall, Friar John, Charlemain and myself watch the comings and goings in a companiable silence. I, for one, have never seen bread cooked inside before, and I have only ever seen portable bread ovens in London. There is something rather magical about the togetherness of the friars and how they work in unison without speaking. The peace is soon broken, though, as Ned, Davy, Owain, Alard, Peter, Morris and the rest of the retinue enters. Laying down their cloaks, they make themselves comfortable and I suspect settled for the night, although I know that Morris and Davy tend to sleep with Liege and Freemantle in the stables, and Ned and Peter will sleep at my door. Far from being put off by the austerity, I rather like it. It is true and honest. Bowls of pottage are served to all, before the bread is broken and shared. The pottage is thick and tasty, and even though the bacon is sparce, it adds to the delicious flavour.

Once everything has been eaten and cleared away, I ask Friar John if it would be possible for me to view Duke Richard's wooden effigy that lies in the chapel.

"Of course, the chapel has been prepared for your visit. A cushioned chair has been placed just inside the door and your privacy guaranteed by the addition of a wooden screen. Please take as much time as you need. The friars will not disturb you."

Grateful for such thoughtfulness, I rise and prepare to leave. With this, Charlemain beckons Ned over and bids me a good night. "Dearest Bethany, I will see you in the morning. My old bones are weary and sleep beckons."

I bend and gently kiss Charlemain on the forehead before leaving.

Outside, the air is crisp and the snow is falling. Taking my arm, Ned carefully guides me through the precinct to the chapel door. "I'll wait for you here, Bethany."

Inside the chapel of St Francis and St Mary Magdalen, the candles burn brightly and night is turned into day. Sweet-smelling herbs burn alongside incense and beeswax tapers. From the other side of the wooden screen, I can hear the friars chanting, rhythmically repeating the same words over and over again. Offering up their prayers and using their voices to praise the Lord at the same time. I take my seat and prepare to look inside the coffin, which sits beneath a beautifully woven majesty cloth depicting Christ in Judgement.

The chapel feels very different to that of Pontefract and a sense of peace washes over me. I allow myself to remember Duke Richard. Not in death, but how he was in life. His face, his smile and the time that we spent together in conversation. How he always cared about others and how he put the needs of his family, friends, retainers and tenants first. His loyalty to King Henry VI. His hurt at having his counsel ignored. His sense of frustration at being banished, especially when false traitors remained by the king's side.

Deciding that the time is right, I rise up and walk tentatively towards the coffin. Standing still, I look directly in front of me and take a deep breath, before looking down. Immediately, I realise that I need not have worried, as the delicately painted wooden effigy of Duke Richard is beautiful. His eyes are open and they gaze towards Heaven, where he now resides. His cheeks have a rosy glow and his lips are perfectly shaped. He is wearing a crimson robe, which is edged with ermine and adorned with seed pearls, and above his head is a small golden crown with a single sapphire. Both his robes and the crown are exactly the same as those at Pontefract Castle. I reach out and touch his face gently. Running my finger along his cheek, I then follow his jawline, before I trace the shape of his lips. The wood is warm to the touch and, in a strange way, almost lifelike. Sitting once more, I contemplate the treachery of Lady Eleanor and Eva de Mortain, and I wonder if Thomas Stanley knows of their arrest and incarceration yet, and if he does, what he will do. I then contemplate the abduction of the king's brothers. Hopefully, they are safe and sound.

I close my eyes and begin to pray for strength, protection and good fortune in my mission. Standing to leave, I curtsy and blow a kiss in the direction of Duke Richard's coffin. Choosing not to look again, I leave with a sense of eagerness for the next leg of the journey.

Watling Street Awaits

At first light, I wash, dress and pack hastily in readiness for Ned's knock at the door. Outside, the snow has stopped and I can see the retinue of Sir William Herbert preparing the baggage train. As expected, Ned knocks on the door. However, he is accompanied by Alard, which is rather odd. Rubbing his hands together, Ned looks in fine form.

"Good morning, Bethany, did you sleep well?"

"Oh yes, I slept far deeper than of late and, to be honest, for the first time in weeks, I felt no fear at all. Even though we are nearing the most dangerous part of our mission, I feel nothing apart from anticipation. When I was in the chapel yesterday, I had time to really think. To decide on a plan of action. It's like everything has fallen into place."

On hearing this, Alard produces a small scroll from inside his cloak. "Mistress, I have something to show you."

Taking the scroll, I untie the red and gold ribbon that binds it, before gently unrolling it. To my surprise, the scroll contains no words, just a mass of straight lines drawn in ink. Turning the scroll this way and that, I inspect it quizzically before looking at Alard. Alard, taking it from my hands, looks equally confused.

"Alard, where did you get this?"

"From Lady Eleanor's chest. I took the liberty of going through her belongings once she was safely under lock and key. It was wrapped up in a very fine piece of linen, which was embroidered with the crest of Richard, Earl of Warwick, and then stuffed into the very bottom of the chest."

Looking once more, I wonder whether it could be some sort of map, before passing it over to Ned for his opinion.

On closer inspection, Ned announces, "Well, I never. Look here. I'm sure that I can see a very faint 'N' scratched into the top of the parchment. Surely it must stand for north and, if that's the case, this cross could relate to the High Cross junction where the Fosse Way crosses Watling Street."

Standing together in thoughtful silence, we are joined by Morris. "The baggage train is ready, and Liege and Fremantle are all prepared. Shall we leave before the Fosse Way becomes too busy?"

Taking the parchment back from Ned, Alard asks Morris for his opinion. "Yes, it would be good to get on the road as quickly as possible, but, Morris, please could you have a look at this first and let us have your thoughts?"

Turning it around, Morris also inspects the parchment for signs. "What have we here then? It looks like some sort of map and a secret code to me. You see that 'N' at the top, and the collection of lines in the middle? Well, they look like north and High Cross. Then, the lines below look like a 'W' enclosed in a box. Then this cross and the wavy line off to the left looks like the position of Leamington Priors church to the south of the River Leam. I've seen something like this before, I just don't know where." Scratching his head, Morris tries to remember. "I'm sorry, but I just can't remember. Where did you find it?"

Alard, halfway through his explanation to Morris, is interrupted abruptly by Ned.

"Sorry, Alard, but it's just come to me, and I must tell you at once. I've just remembered where I saw this before. It was at Towton Hall. Morris, can't you remember? Warwick drew similar patterns to this in the gravel with the heel of his boot. I thought that it was odd at the time."

"By Christ, you're right! Warwick must have been passing on information to someone, but who could that someone be?" Alard, looking pale, continues, "I'm ahead of you there. Warwick was obviously passing a message onto Eva de Mortain, who then committed it to parchment. If only we knew what it meant."

Joined by Davy and Peter, we all try to break the secret code with little success. Looking at the sky, Morris suggests that we think about it on the road and we set off in search of Charlemain, who we find already seated in the back of the cart.

"Bethany, my dear, are you well? I was wondering where everyone had got to."

As the cart pulls away, I hand the parchment to Charlemain, who immediately goes white. "Where did you get this?"

"Alard found it in Lady Eleanor's chest, wrapped in a piece of fine linen, which was embroidered with the Earl of Warwick's crest."

"That makes sense; it looks like the route to Warwick Castle, with two stopping places. The first being High Cross and the second being Weston under Wetherley. We must be careful. I sense a trap has been laid for us at Weston and they seek to box us in."

Alard, who is walking at our side, immediately springs into action. "That settles it then. We'll leave the Fosse Way and travel to Warwick via Coventry. Morris, do you know the way to Coventry?"

"That I do, Alard. We'll head across country to Monks Kirby and then enter Coventry through the Cook Gate. Let me lead the way."

As the hours pass, the icy cold steadily seeps into everyone. I snuggle into Charlemain and pull up the sheepskin for added comfort. Looking into Charlemain's eyes, I am concerned as he has a vacant, almost lost expression.

As the light begins to fade, Morris announces, "We're nearly there now, but who knows where we'll sleep. No one will be expecting us."

To this, Alard just shrugs. Perhaps he's trying to formulate a plan in his head, or maybe he's just as concerned as Morris, but unwilling to speak of his concerns.

As we enter the village of Monks Kirby, Morris – attempting to be positive – informs us that we have just entered via a street named Bonds End. "Now, this is an interesting place. It's an informal boundary marking the place where the bondsmen of the village become free to create their own wealth."

I consider the word 'free' and its many meanings, but am rudely woken from my thoughts when we are flagged down by a young page, who is wearing very fine outer garments and a baldric made of pale-blue linen. Fearful of an ambush, Morris draws Liege and Fremantle to an immediate halt and all the men draw their daggers. Ned, Owain, Davy and Sir William's retinue surround the cart.

Charlemain, having regained his demeanour, clings onto my arm and bids that I sit completely still and silent. "Do not speak, Bethany. Who knows what's happening? But fear not, for I will protect you with my life if need be."

At this, tears begin to roll down my cheeks. Dear Charlemain; how I love him with all my heart. Quickly regaining my composure, I gaze down on the young page, who has walked around to my side of the cart. He is shaking violently.

"Welcome. Please may I enquire if you are Lady Harsyck of South Acre?"

Surprised to be addressed in such a manner, I nod in the direction of Peter and Alard, who immediately step in between the page and the cart. Peter is the first to speak and his imposing presence appears to unnerve the page even further. "Yes, we're the baggage train of Lady Harsyck, but, more importantly, who are you and how did you know who we are?"

Gulping before speaking, the page pulls a sealed scroll from his satchel. "Please take this. It was delivered to the manor house of the Feilding Family at Newnham Paddox earlier today. We were advised of your arrival and we have made provision for you all; not at the manor house, but at the Carthusian Abbey, which is aligned to the deceased Thomas Mowbray and his ancestors, the Dukes of Norfolk. You will be safe and secure inside the abbey walls. Alas, there are only two priests in residence to take care of you, but there are provisions aplenty. Bread, cheese, ale, firewood and charcoal. You will not go hungry, thirsty or be cold. I have been assured by your private messenger that the contents of this scroll will provide you with more details, but I do not have any knowledge of its contents and neither do I wish to know. It is enough that I have completed my duty in a satisfactory manner."

Alard, taking the scroll, breaks the seal before reading its contents over and over again. Then, with a look of relief, he places the scroll into a concealed pocket within his cape. Looking up, he begins to question the page. "What is your name?"

"I am Jeremiah of Denbigh. My father was a Welshman, loyal to the deceased Richard, Duke of York. He died at the Battle of Wakefield a few months ago. I am alone now, without any close relatives, but I am grateful to the Dukes of Norfolk who have provided me with a roof over my head and food in my stomach."

"Well, Jeremiah, you have carried out your duties to perfection. Are you happy here? Or do you have ambitions of leaving the manor of Newnham Paddox? I only ask as we could do with a page of such excellent quality."

Jeremiah stops shaking for the first time and smiles. "Oh, how I would love to leave the manor and travel with Lady Harsyck's baggage train. Word has it that Lady Harsyck is the most devout and true Yorkist and one of the Mortimer line. It would be such an honour."

"Well, I'll send word to the Feilding family in the morning and see what they say. In the meantime, would you be kind enough to direct us to the abbey?"

An excited Jeremiah nods and beams with joy, especially when Morris offers his hand to him and pulls him up onto the cart, saying, "Come on, boy, you ride next to old Morris. I'll teach you a thing or two."

With laughter, we pull away and dread to think what Morris intends on teaching Jeremiah!

The abbey is somewhat faded, but secure and well-stocked – just as Jeremiah said it would be. Luckily, Sir William's men have bought along canvases, which can be used to create shelters. Immediately, they begin to dig small holes and erect wooden poles. As seasoned campaigners, the men are unfazed by the necessity of such work.

The elder of them calls out to Jeremiah for help. "Lad, come here! I need your help. Hold that pole while I grab the rope."

Jeremiah, happy to help, does as he is told. Once the rope is securely tied, Charlemain and I climb down from the cart and sit by the newly laid fire. I watch as the purple flames grow and turn orange, dancing with increased intensity. In the distance, two priests approach from a side door of the abbey. They appear flustered and unaccustomed to visitors.

Running to greet them, Jeremiah grabs their hands and pulls them towards the fire. "Come, let me introduce you to Lady Harsyck."

In the manner of a father, the eldest priest rubs Jeremiah's head and looks on him with great affection. "You're a good boy, Jem, but you really do need to control your emotions a little better. We are all friends here, but the world can be a dangerous place. Please remember to be a little more guarded in future and cover your emotions."

Nodding enthusiastically, Jem can't help but recount our meeting and Alard's offer of leaving the manor. "Yes, Father, you're right. I'm just so excited and surely it won't hurt to be happy here with you, within the confines of the abbey."

Smiling back, the elderly father relents and agrees. "Yes, it's fine to be exuberant in this House of the Lord."

As the fathers approach, Charlemain and I stand to greet them.

"Welcome to this House of the Carthusians, I am Father Gerald and this is Father Denis."

Extending my hand to greet them both, I am alarmed to notice that the younger priest, Father Denis, has no left hand. Trying but failing to cover my shock in time, Father Denis smiles and comments, "Do not be alarmed, my dear. The loss of my hand does not disturb me. I lost it many years ago, when I was on campaign in Agincourt."

On hearing of Agincourt, I immediately think of Good Duke Humphrey and my family.

Father Denis, pre-empting my question, states, "Yes, my dear, I accompanied Good Duke Humphrey and I know of your family, the Mortimers."

I cannot help but wonder how Father Denis knows so much, but I decide not to ask at this time, as Father Gerald's conversation with Charlemain is ending and I wish to listen in.

"We have prepared four rooms for your party. One for yourself, one for Lady Harsyck and two for members of your immediate retinue. I believe that Ned and Peter would like to rest close by – although, in reality, you are all safe."

Morris is the first of our party to reappear. Having fed, watered and groomed Liege and Fremantle, he now sits by the fire with Jem by his side. "Now, lad, you'll be sleeping outside my door tonight. It'll teach you how to nap and be alert at the same time – a very valuable lesson to learn and one that I learnt when I was about your age. I was page to Sir Edmund Mortimer."

I look up in shock. Morris, noting my shock, laughs and says, "I thought that would grab your attention, Mistress."

As promised, our rooms have been prepared. Leaving Charlemain at the threshold, I kiss his hands before leaving him and entering alone. Immediately, I make my way over to the window, eager to see how the encampment has grown. I note that quite a few fires now burn and that many canvases have been erected.

A knock at the door startles me and I call out, "Who's there?"

Alard responds, "Forgive me for disturbing you, but I wondered if you would like to accompany me to the manuscripts room. I hear that they create exquisitely crafted illuminated books here within the abbey and I thought that they may have some spare parchment, as I need to write a letter to the Fielding Family."

Opening the door, I am more than happy to accompany Alard. Walking side by side, we make haste along a covered walkway to the manuscripts room. The roof protects us from the snow, which refuses to stop falling. I notice that the wind has picked up and I wrap my cloak tightly around me. Stopping at a heavily carved oak door, Alard turns the bronze handle and the door creaks opens. Inside, there are two very large desks, one on either side of the hearth. Both are positioned directly under large windows. Looking around, Alard finds a piece of parchment, a quill and some plain black ink, before taking a seat at the desk on the left.

While Alard sits to write, I stroll over to the other desk and take a look. Upon it is a mixing palette; each aperture being full to the brim with brightly coloured pigments, a selection of brushes and two small bowls of water. One, I presume, is for mixing and the others for cleaning the brushes. There are also numerous scraps of fine linen, two wooden tools – both resembling wooden quills – a small palette knife and a large white goose feather. If I am right, the wooden tools and palette knife are used to apply the flattened wafer-thin silver or gold, and the feather is used to both smooth the metals onto the parchment and to brush away any excess. Knowing that a sticky substance is used to fix everything in place, I am not surprised to find a collection of eggs close by, as the sticky substance used is more often than not made from the white sticky residue of egg whites, with the addition of a little earwax to prevent bubbles from occurring. However, I do not linger on the thought of collecting and using earwax.

Alard, having finished his letter, joins me. "Well, I'll have this delivered to the Fielding's first thing tomorrow morning. Jem is made of solid stuff and would be a very valuable addition to our baggage train. Few pages would have been brave enough to deliver a message with such eloquence when surrounded by many drawn blades."

Nodding in agreement, I also comment on his bravery. I also take this opportunity to ask Alard about our private messenger, to which Alard just smiles and replies that it is late, and we should be getting back. Not wanting to push the issue, I rest in the knowledge that Alard will tell me when the time is right.

Back inside my room, with Peter napping outside, I remove my cloak and lay it across my mattress. It will provide added warmth in the night. Then, I remove my coif and outer kirtle before climbing into bed. The linen is smooth and cool against my skin. Lying still, I listen to the dying embers of the fire in the hearth and long for Pip. I would have no need for fire if Pip was here with me, as his body would keep me warm. Alas, that is not the case, so I shut my eyes and drift off immediately.

Waking from a long deep sleep, I can hear excited squealing outside. It would appear that the Fieldings have responded immediately to Alard's letter and, now, an overexcited Jem is jumping up and down on the spot, while bidding that Alard open the scroll straight away. Alard, trying hard to cover his anxiety and remain calm, requests that rather than hang around, Jem and Peter should fetch a large jug of hot water, a bowl and clean linen.

"There's no point hanging around here. I'm not going to open the scroll just yet. I have things to do. Now, go and get the water, bowl and linen for Mistress Bethany and take it to her room. Jem, you are to wait by the threshold, while Peter enters and relights the fire. Then, you are both to stand guard outside the door until told otherwise."

Jem, returning to service mode, takes his instructions and does what he is told. Peter, on the other hand, hangs back to speak to Alard. "You look concerned. Is there a problem?"

"No, Peter, I'm just wary of the answer within this scroll. It could destroy Jem's dreams of escaping this village."

"Well, there's no time like the present. I'll keep Jem busy, while you read the contents of that scroll. Then, if the answer is positive, let me know by removing your cap. If the answer is negative, keep your cap on and take off your cloak."

I hesitate by the window and look for the secret sign. To my relief, as Jem and Peter pass, Alard removes his cap and smiles before replacing it. Grasping my cloak, I wrap it around my shoulders and wait for the knock at the door.

After washing and dressing, I pack my trunk and emerge in search of bread and cheese. Ned is the first to greet me.

"Good morning, Bethany, I hope that you had a pleasant night. I slept like a log, safe in the knowledge that both Peter and Jem were on guard."

"Me too – surprisingly the room retained its heat and I was most comfortable."

Together, we head off in the direction of the fire, only to be greeted by one of Sir William's retainers. On seeing me, the small thin man prepares a seat for me by the fire. I smile and acknowledge him, but I feel a sense of unease. His facial features appear familiar to me and not in a good way. His head is rather too small for his body and he has a mass of blond wiry hair that sticks out at all angles. His eye sockets are sunken and his eyes are dull. Seated, I beckon to Owain to join me and Ned. Looking around, I make sure that no one is close enough to hear, then I begin, "I am fearful. I know that face from somewhere. I just don't know where. Please keep a watch on that man. I'm sure that our paths have crossed before."

Immediately alarmed, Ned and Owain ask me to try and remember. I close my eyes and concentrate as hard as possible. I'm almost convinced that I saw that face on the way to Walsingham, but it's no good. Opening my eyes, I take another long look at the man, before closing my eyes again. This time, though, I concentrate on letting my mind be free. Then, all of a sudden, it comes to me. I open my eyes, before leaning forward and grasping both Owain and Ned's wrists. Beads of sweat begin to form around the rim of my coif and my body shakes violently within.

"That man – he's surely the son of the beggar woman who tried to blind me with her long nails on the road to

Walsingham. Look at his hands; they're not only the same size and shape, but they bare the same birthmark. A dark plum-coloured horseshoe. He's a traitor, I'm sure of it. He must be arrested and detained immediately."

With stealth, Owain stands and walks away calmly in the direction of Sir William's head retainer. With a deep Welsh drawl, Sir Allen begins, "Welcome, Owain, what can I do for you this fine morning?"

"Ah, well, I don't quite know how to say this, Sir Allen, but we are certain that one of your number is related to a beggar that tried to blind Lady Harsyck on the road to Walsingham. They bear the same birthmark and we are sorely concerned."

Stroking his white beard, it is obvious that Sir Allen is unaware of the individual that Owain speaks of. "Without turning, please describe him to me."

"Well, he's not overly tall; his head is rather too small for his body; he has a mass of blond wiry hair that sticks out at all angles; and his eye sockets are sunken."

"Owain, I do not recall anyone of that description within my ranks. Does he wear my colours?"

"Let me go and check."

"No, let's go together."

Within a few minutes, Ned and I are joined by Sir Allen and Owain. Sitting next to me, Sir Allen leans in close before pretending to warm his hands by the fire.

"Do not be alarmed, Lady Harsyck, but I need you and Ned to stand up slowly and return to your room. When you get there, lock the door and do not leave until I tell you that you can. The man that you speak of is not one of my number, even although he wears my sash. All of my men have been instructed to prepare the carts and assist the holy fathers."

Standing, I force my legs to move. However, before we can make it to the safety of my room, history repeats itself and we are attacked – not by the blond man with wiry hair, but by the same bald man that attacked me on the road to Walsingham. His eyes are black and guarded, his jowls are yellow and saggy, and his mouth is twisted in anger. I just cannot work out where he appeared from. On his head, he wears a rather odd wide-brimmed hat, which is covered in a greasy film.

I scream out, "Help! Somebody, please help!"

With no option but to try and make it to safety, I grasp my kirtle and begin to run, before I hear a howling noise behind me. Stopping to look, I am frozen to the spot, as the bald man writhes on the ground with an arrow through his upper torso. Blood is spurting out at an alarming rate, before the sound of his departure fills the air. In a blind panic, I scour the scene for the man with sunken eyes. He, too, lies flat out with an arrow through his upper torso. Feeling sick, I slump to the ground.

Within seconds, Ned and Owain are by my side, and Morris and Davy draw the cart alongside me. Liege, realising that something is wrong, nuzzles his nose into my neck, before standing in such a way as to protect me. I can feel his hot breathe on my face and the cold snow seeping through the fabric of my kirtle.

Within no time at all, I am picked up and placed in the back of the cart. Lying on my back, I can see nothing but the sky – however, I am aware of the rest of the baggage train running to our assistance and Jem's voice calling out, "I got them! I got them both!"

Sitting up, I catch sight of Jem, who has been picked up by Peter of Pontefract. Peter is swirling him around, high in the air, while the men of the baggage train salute him.

I call out, "Morris, what's happening? Was it Jem who shot them both?"

"Yes, Mistress, he got them both through the heart. He's an amazing archer, especially for one so young."

Realising that I am lying in the back of the cart, Jem runs to my side. "Mistress, you are safe. God be praised. I was so frightened that I would miss them both and that they would kill you. I've never hit a moving target before and now I've hit two in one go."

Unable to control the shock, I begin to sob. If only Pip were here. I wish that I was in his arms.

Within seconds, Jem vaults into the cart and begins to cradle me in his arms. "Please, Mistress, please don't cry."

Looking up into Jem's face, a feeling of immense sadness washes over me. I have everyone and he has no one.

Sitting up, I wait until we are joined by Alard before speaking. "Jem, thank you for saving my life. You are mature beyond your years. Lord Harsyck, my husband, would be so proud of your actions."

Jem, thinking fast, replies, "Well, if I became your page, I'm sure to meet him at some point."

Laughter fills the air as Morris responds, "You tyke, you. Come on – come and sit with old Morris upfront. We're leaving now and as part of your duties as page, you are now the official lookout."

Jem, realising the significance, looks from side to side. "Thank you, all. I'll never let you down."

Accompanied by Charlemain, I take my seat before nodding in response. "Dearest Jem, we know that you will never let us down and I want you to know that we'll never let you down either."

Then, followed by the rest of the baggage train, we leave Monks Kirby and the two dead bodies behind us for our last resting place before Warwick Castle. The mighty town of Coventry.

The Spires of Coventry

A sense of relief floods over all of us when the numerous wooden and stone spires of Coventry come into view, with all five standing proud above the crenelated town walls. God be praised that we have made it this far without being ambushed. To our left, the River Sherbourne meanders off into the distance and to our right stands a mighty gatehouse. I have never seen anything like it before. It is made of dark red sandstone, has a slightly rounded arch and is one storey high. The ground floor has no windows, whereas the first storey has one large central window with a single stone mullion running from top to bottom.

Morris, noting my interest, says, "Yes, it's a very fine gatehouse, Mistress. It's called the Cook Street Gate. Coventry is well known for having twelve gates, with this being the main one. For the life of me, I cannot understand the need for so many, but it's probably down to the internal conflicts within the town. You see, for hundreds of years, this town has been split into two. For as long as anyone can remember, there's always been conflict between the Benedictine Priory of St Mary's and the local Earls of Cheshire. Both owning half of Coventry and both trying to impose their will on the other side."

Thinking for a while, I ponder on the nature of Coventry before speaking, "Morris, is Coventry Yorkist or Lancastrian?"

"Well, that's a story in itself. Surely you have heard of the Parliament of Devils a couple of years ago?"

"Yes, Morris, I have heard of it, but Pip sought to shield me from the details of it at the time."

"That makes sense. It was the vilest attempt by Queen Margaret and her followers to trap and kill all the Yorkists, in particular Duke Richard, King Edward (then Earl of March), Edmund Rutland and Richard Salisbury."

We all cross ourselves at this and I immediately feel a lump in my throat. Holding back my tears, I ask Morris to continue.

"Well, a parliament was called and an Act was eventually passed. The Act stated that, in total, twenty-seven Yorkists were to be executed and their deaths were to be pronounced as 'legal deaths'. The Act also stated that not only were the Yorkists to be killed but their lands and goods were to be forfeited to the Crown, meaning that Queen Margaret would get everything." My blood begins to boil and my face begins to redden in anger. "But that's not the end of it, Mistress. After the Act was read out, a good number of Coventry folk, led by an unknown leader, rose up in defiance. They risked death and destruction to speak out on behalf of Duke Richard and the Yorkists. Offended by the lack of a fair trial and with their good morals compromised, they openly condemned the Act as a malicious Act, and they took up arms in aid of the Yorkists. Most Coventry souls being free, and a mixture of merchants and traders, took it upon themselves to prepare armour and supplies for the Yorkists."

Hearing this, my mood begins to lighten. Alard, having heard us, approaches my side of the cart and walks besides me. "Morris is right."

On hearing this, Morris laughs. "I know, I'm always right."

Alard, rubbing his forehead, continues, "However, I'm still concerned that Lancastrian sympathisers are all around. Our scouts have spotted a great number of the queen's men. They are masquerading as traders and are centred around the marketplace, in particular Potter Row, Cook Street and Great and Little Butcheries. They appear to have taken refuge in the prior's half of the town. Prior Gosforth, having nothing to do with them, sent word to King Edward weeks ago. He petitioned the king and asked for his help in removing them from the town, but Edward feels that, at the moment, it's best not to say or do anything. Just to keep watch and monitor their movements. To this end, Edward has contacted a number of his loyal supporters in Coventry and has asked them to be on the alert and to contact him should they hear anything."

With this, Charlemain asks, "Alard, I am concerned. Are we safe?"

"Yes, Charlemain, we have an armed guard and, as far as I'm aware, the queen's men do not have the capacity to take on an entire baggage train. Sir William Catesby is expecting us, and I hear that he has been instrumental in clearing both the Guildhall and the Cathedral of St Mary's. We will take up residence in the Guildhall overnight and the baggage train will set up camp in the cathedral grounds. As both locations are linked via a narrow lane, we can secure a vast area with the men that we have."

Jem, leaping into action, offers to keep watch with his bow and arrows. "I'll keep watch, Alard. Please let me be a lookout."

"No lad, you will have a far greater role than lookout. You will accompany Peter both day and night wherever he goes. You will act as a private guard for Mistress Bethany and Charlemain. Protecting both with your life, if necessary."

Peter rolls his eyes at the thought of Jem's enthusiasm, while Jem straightens his back and holds himself proud.

As we roll into the Cook Street Gate, we pass tanners and furriers hard at work. The smell is nauseating – a mixture of urine and blood. I clasp my hands to my face, blocking my nose and momentarily holding my breath.

Morris, seemingly unaffected, laughs and breaths in deeply. "Aye, that's the smell of Coventry all right, but we'll soon be in the sweeter-smelling air of the earl's half. Once we're past the market and the narrow surrounding streets, we'll encounter the larger houses of the town and, if my memory serves me correctly, they all have extremely large gardens and storage barns."

Having regained my sense of composure and wishing to have something to take my mind off the smell, I ask Morris to describe the earl's half in more detail.

"Well, it is the upper-class end of Coventry, where all of the wealthy merchants have their homes and businesses. For the largest part, they are mainly weavers and cloth merchants. This area is exceptionally well known for a type of broadcloth that they produce. It's called Coventry blue and it's dyed with woad, which has been imported from the Low Countries through the port of Bristol. No one really knows why, but the blue never fades."

Looking down at my kirtle, I say, "Morris, do you think that we could buy some Coventry blue broadcloth? I really could do with a new outer kirtle."

"Buy cloth, Mistress? No, you are Lady Harsyck and, as such, we will make arrangements for you to have a special gown and matching coif made for you." Morris leans to the right and calls out, "Ned, where are you, lad?"

"I am here, Morris. Just give me a few minutes and you will have my full attention." As promised, Ned soon bounds into view. "And what can I do for you, my dear friend?"

"Ned, you're a popinjay if ever I knew one. Could you arrange for the local seamstresses to make a special gown and coif for Mistress Bethany tonight?"

"Yes, my friend and I know exactly where to go. I'll take two of Sir Allen's men with me and meet you later at the Guildhall with seamstresses and cloth aplenty. They'll be honoured to create a gown for Lady Harsyck and baldricks for her private retainers and baggage train. Then we'll look a sight to behold when we arrive at Warwick Castle. Pip would expect us to outshine the others, and King Edward has provided most generously for our mission." He bounds off with a mighty bow.

Morris, shaking his head, comments, "I knew that the thought of new clothes would ignite Ned's enthusiasm. I wouldn't be surprised if we don't all end up with new shoes and hose to boot."

Laughing, I relax and listen to Morris as he calls out the street names as we pass. "Over there is Gosford Street and Earl Street, where the clothiers and drapers reside, and then we have Well Street, West Orchard and Spon Street, where the tailors and fullers ply their trades. On the left is Catesby

Street, where Sir William Catesby lives. He's a true and loyal Yorkist, but – if what I hear is true – he's a bit of a recluse and he never receives visitors to his house. Last but not least, we are nearing the great Cathedral of St Mary. It grew out of the Benedictine Abbey of St Mary's and is a sight to behold."

Astonished at Morris's knowledge of the area, I wonder how he knows so much.

As we approach the gates of the cathedral, I look up in wonder at the three large wooden spires. One belongs to the central tower, while two are located at the west end. As we pass by, I notice that we are flanked by parish churches on either side. To the left, Holy Trinity and to the right, St Michael's. Both have exquisite masonry and are, no doubt, endowed by the wealthy cloth merchants, who live in their shadows. However, both churches are completely outshone when the cathedral gates are opened, and the west front of the cathedral comes into full view. It's magnificent! There are seemingly hundreds of small statues, each sitting neatly within moulded niches. I have never seen the likes of it before.

Once we are all safely ensconced inside, the large wooden gates are shut and bolted behind us, before a group of brothers secure the gates even further with the use of two iron bars that sit inside specially created apertures of the surrounding stonework.

Charlemain looks pale and I am concerned. "Charlemain, are you well?"

"Oh, Bethany, how I feel my age nowadays, but I'll feel as good as new after a nice long nap."

Once down from the cart, I survey the cathedral gardens and notice that the trees are starting to spring into life.

White and pink blossom wave about in the cool air, but my attention is soon bought back to the present when I hear the prior approach.

"God be praised that you are safe. Mistress Bethany, please let me introduce myself. I am Prior Gosforth and I stand here in place of Dean Heywood, who has been called away to our sister cathedral of Lichfield. Dean Haywood is overseeing the work on St Chad's new stone shrine. Up until now, St Chad's right arm has been kept in a portable shrine and his skull in a painted box, but neither are secure enough, now that many hundreds of pilgrims visit us each year, and our dear bishop is in Westminster, overseeing the preparations for glorious King Edward IV's coronation. I hear that the work will take many more months to complete, but I am assured that everything will be in place for the 28th June, when the sun will shine on our new king."

To that, everyone in the vicinity calls out, "God save King Edward IV. Hurrah!"

Taking Charlemain's arm, we follow Prior Gosforth in the direction of the Chapter House. "Oh, there's so much to show you and so little time. I understand that you, my dear Charlemain, would like to retire immediately, so I have had a chamber in the Guildhall prepared. A fire has been lit, a comfy bed awaits, as does a plate of cheese and bread. You will also find a jug of wine to fortify you."

Charlemain nods in grateful recognition and kisses me on both cheeks before he departs with Davy. I can hear Owain's footsteps behind me, along with those of Peter and Jem. Owain takes Charlemain's place and holds my arm.

Bishop Gosforth begins once more. "Come all, let's go inside. I have something to show you."

Inside the Chapter House, we have to divert immediately to our left to avoid stepping on a large stone tomb, which sits directly inside the door. It is decorated with an incised cross and a carving of a church window. Bowing in reverence and crossing himself, Prior Gosforth explains that this is the final resting place of our most celebrated residents. John of Coventry and his descendant, John Thornton, were both glaziers of the highest order and both have left behind many works of art for us to cherish. John of Coventry having been commissioned by King Edward III to work at both Westminster Abbey and St George's Chapel, Windsor, and then John Thornton, who was commissioned by Walter Skirlaw, the late Bishop of Durham, and the blessed Archbishop Richard Scrope to create the Great East Window of York Minster. Both were amazing artists and, as such, they were both awarded the great honour of being buried just inside the Chapter House door.

After respectfully crossing ourselves, I ask Prior Gosforth to describe the Great East Window at York Minster.

"Oh, it's a joy to behold. The window tells the story of the beginning and the end; the Creation and the Revelation. Among various historical figures, there are angels, apostles prophets, patriarchs, martyrs and saints, along with twenty-seven scenes from the Old Testament, and finally a scene from the Apocalypse." At this, Prior Gosforth gets rather excited. "Please, come with me. I long to show you our Apocalypse painting. It's one of our great treasures."

As we walk across the Chapter House, I notice the fine brown glazed tiles upon which we walk upon. They are decorated not only with the shield of Edward the Confessor, but small birds akin to sparrows. These birds are also depicted throughout the beautiful stained-glass windows that surround us.

As we leave the Chapter House behind us and emerge into the body of the cathedral, I immediately catch my breath. Again, the Apocalypse painting is unlike anything that I have ever seen before. It is surrounded by whitewashed walls and it completely dominates the eye. The story that it tells is of repentance and of living a good life, before it is too late. If we do not live a good and pure life, we will descend into the eternal fires of Hell. Diverting my eyes from the dancing Devil, I notice that the floor consists entirely of green glazed tiles, which glisten in the candlelight. However, I am bought back to the present on hearing a squeal of delight. We all look towards Jem, who immediately blushes.

"Oh, please forgive me. I am so sorry. I must remember my position as page to Lady Harsyck, but I've never been in a cathedral before, and I just can't believe how lucky I am to be here." He looks at the floor in embarrassment, until Owain puts a brotherly arm around his shoulder.

"Don't worry, Jem, we're all friends here – just be a little more guarded in future. Why don't you take Lady Harsyck's arm? I will walk behind you both with Peter."

Jem extends his hand in the same way that Owain had, before he slips his arm in mine. Looking down on him, I realise just how small and frail he is. Returning my attention to Prior Gosforth, we walk through the nave to the chancel before descending the steps into the crypt. The crypt is yet another masterpiece and is separated into three sections. Each section having a finely carved and vaulted ceiling, with floral ceiling bosses and golden crosses. Prior Gosforth, holding his hand up, stops us directly in front of a pair of heavy dark-blue velvet curtains. I notice that they hang from a wooden pole, which is decorated at each end with wooden flowers. Stepping forward, Prior Gosforth opens the curtains to reveal a spectacular mural. This time, we all catch our breaths, and a stunned silence descends.

Painted on the wall, there are four heads, three of which are adorned with golden crowns. The gold is sparkling in the candlelight. Below the heads, there are scenes from the baptism of Jesus. I just can't believe my eyes, as this painting depicts a passage taken from my favourite book of the Bible, St Matthew. Coincidentally, Duke Richard was born on the Feast of St Matthew. I cross myself and, for a moment, I picture Duke Richard's beautiful face, smiling at me, before regaining my focus and looking to the furthest corner of the painting where the dove of peace sits upon an olive branch. The white enamelled dove is showing the way to Heaven and the ascent to God. It has a band of gold at his neck and two golden feet. The candlelight adds a magical quality, with rays of light descending from Heaven.

Prior Gosforth is the first to speak. "I can see that you are all as enthralled with the mural as we are. It was painted nearly one hundred years ago and is very fragile, hence we keep it covered."

Regaining my voice, I release myself from Jem's tiny but muscular arm and step forward to take a closer look. "Prior Gosforth, we are honoured that you have shown the mural to us. It is the most beautiful painting that I have ever seen."

Prior Gosforth beams with joy before drawing the curtains once more and inviting us to follow him to the Guildhall. "I am sure that Alard has already told you, but you are all to stay at the Guildhall tonight. It's not very far."

Outside, we cross a small lane that is guarded at both ends by Sir Allen's and Sir William's retainers. They smile as we pass. I feel a sense of comfort at their presence. Outside of the Guildhall, Alard, Davy, Ned and Morris greet us. As we enter the doorway, I can detect a strong scent of mint on the air. My mind begins to race. Is Pip close by? Covertly, I look around and see a hooded and cloaked figure just beyond the entrance. However, the figure vanishes before I can get a good look. Not wanting to give away Pip's presence to all, I open my cloak and fiddle with my heron broach. Alard, noticing this, smiles and this is all I need to alert me to Pip's presence. I wonder if he will come to me tonight. Surely not, with both Jem and Peter standing guard.

Inside the Guildhall, I am introduced to Sir William Catesby. He is a tall, robust-looking man with red weather-beaten cheeks, who bows low before me. "I am pleased to meet you, Lady Harsyck. I knew your father-in-law, Sir Roger Harsyck, very well. We campaigned together many years ago. He was a true and loyal gentleman. I hear that his son is of the same mould and that he loyally served Richard, Duke of York, to the bitter end at the Battle of Wakefield. Again, I campaigned with Richard, Duke of York, many years ago and never was there a finer commander and leader of men than him, but I should not reminisce, as my heart breaks every time I think of Duke Richard and Edmund Rutland." We all cross ourselves. "Please come with me into the hall. The light is fading fast and I had hoped that you should see our stained glass, which was designed and created by John Thornton."

The door is closed and two of Sir Allen's retainers remain outside and two inside. As we walk to the great hall, I ponder on the identity of the Coventry resident who raised up and led a rebellion against the Lancastrians and the decision of the Parliament of Devils and the evil Act, which prescribed certain death for the Yorkists. Perhaps this is the reason that Sir William rarely entertains people within his home. I suspect that it is a Yorkist safe house!

The great hall is just that. The wall at the farthest end is dominated by a rounded arched window, which is comprised of three smaller arched windows. There are two heavy stone mullions in the centre and three delicate stone mullions on either side. Unlike other stained glass, where the base colours are predominantly blue and red, the base colours are yellow and green. In addition, there are a multitude of stained-glass windows along both walls on either side of the hall. These are more delicate in nature, but they share the same base colours.

Walking around the hall in wonder, I notice that all of the windows are peppered with lifelike faces. All seem to share the same facial features; they appear sensitive, with down-turned eyes, unusually small mouths and large noses. Their hair is so real, I feel like I could reach out and touch it. It not only has movement, but delicate streaks of contrasting colours. Looking down, I contemplate the floor. The brown glazed tiles are very similar to those of the Chapter House and, I imagine, the work of the same craftsman. However, they are not adorned with the shield of Edward the Confessor or small birds. These are rather more mosaic in design, with fine borders of dark-brown tiles, encompassing paler blown and cream tiles with designs taken from nature. I can see flowers and leaves, alongside dots and lines.

In the centre of the room, rather than an open hearth, there are arched borders surrounding sixteen very high-status tiles. These have a deeper glaze and shine even brighter in the candlelight. Behind me, there is a large open fireplace with a roaring fire and two arched doors that I presume lead to the kitchens. Delicious smells are emanating and my stomach rumbles.

Prior Gosforth, noting my delight, stands even taller. "Yes, we are truly blessed in Coventry. The land in this area, although not ideal for farming, is perfect for raw materials. We rarely have to order in any clay or stone. In this fine town, we have many Guilds and the Leet to make sure that everything that is produced is of the highest quality."

We are interrupted by the arrival of a young boy. Similar in age and statue to Jem, he stands before us in a fine linen shift and woollen hose. After bowing low to me, he turns and addresses Sir William Catesby, who I suspect he knows very well. If I am not mistaken, he looks to be related and may even be his son.

"Sir William, the food is nearly ready, and Cook Edgar would like to know where you would like it served?"

"I think that we should eat upstairs in the chamber next to the Buttery. Has a fire been lit?"

"Oh yes, we have lit fires in all of the chambers, in readiness for our guests."

"Excellent, Will, please see to it that ten places are set, and that the best chair is placed nearest to the fireplace."

Will nods. "Cook Edgar would also like you to know that he has prepared provisions for all of Lady Harsyck's retainers, and that this will be taken over to the cathedral shortly."

Smiling, Sir William ruffles Will's hair and smiles. "Good work, lad, you're learning fast."

Will bows once more before leaving the hall.

Sir William, turning to us, invites us to take a seat by the fire, while we are waiting for the chamber to be prepared. Warm and comfortable, we happily accept. However, the peace and quiet of the hall is soon broken by the arrival of Ned and over thirty seamstresses. Having reverted to his natural behaviour, Ned is not only playing the shawm and acting the fool, but is dressed the part in his fool's garb.

Alard, looking none too happy, speaks, "I thought that you had left that ridiculous outfit behind at South Acre."

Ned, who is laughing, retorts, "Ah well, you know what thought did, don't you? I never travel without it, as I never know when it will come in handy."

I think to myself that it is very handy indeed as all of the seamstresses appear to be swooning over Ned and, as such, he has them eating out of his hands.

Addressing the seamstresses, Ned introduces me and the party, before he requests that the senior seamstress steps forward. She appears older than the rest and has disformed fingers on both hands. I expect this is due to the nature of her work. She smiles and bows low out of respect, her back appearing too bent to curtsy.

"Welcome, Lady Harsyck, I am Beatrice of Sandal and I am the senior seamstress here. Ned has requested that I make for you a fine Coventry blue gown with flowing arms and silk laces, and that the others make fine baldricks and hose for your entire retinue, and we are more than happy to help. We have many baldricks and hose already in stock, so that's not a problem. We also have linen tunics and linen under kirtles in store, so it's just a case of me measuring you and everyone pulling together."

Grateful for such kindness and intrigued by her name

I ask, "Thank you so much, Beatrice of Sandal, you are most kind. Does the 'Sandal' in your name refer to Sandal Castle?"

"Yes, my lady, and I am proud to say that I was seamstress to both Cecily, Duchess of York, and Richard, Duke of York."

We smile at each other. Sir William, who is also smiling, suggests that we retire to a chamber on the upper floor, so that Beatrice can measure me before we eat.

Climbing the steep stone spiral staircase, Sir William leads the way, while Jem and Peter follow close behind me. I note that Beatrice, who has called forward two of her seamstresses, is supervising the transportation of the blue broadcloth cloth, needles and thread.

Once upstairs in the chamber, I let Beatrice lead me over to the window. The light has almost gone now and I can see the flames burning brightly from the torches in the cathedral grounds. I can also see Sir William's and Sir Allen's men making themselves comfortable for the night and awaiting their refreshments. It always astonishes me just how quickly an encampment can be set up and how it can be dismantled even faster.

At Beatrice's request, I remove my outer kirtle and stand as still as possible. This is a very new experience for me, as I have never had a gown made especially for me. With speed and accuracy, Beatrice measures and cuts many pieces of fabric. They are then pinned into place, before being cut into shape. Working from the shoulders down, my gown miraculously appears. By using great swathes of fabric, Beatrice has created a very full skirt, which is pleated at the waist, a slim bodice and very fashionable sleeves.

"Now, Lady Harsyck, here we come to hardest part. We

need to remove the gown without losing any of the pins. If you just stand still, we will lift your dress over your head."

I do as I am told, for fear of being scratched to pieces. Within no time at all, the gown is off and I am helped into my old kirtle. I look with joy and amazement at my new gown.

"Tonight, we will sew this together, before Bridie and myself create the silk laces. It will be finished before dawn."

With grateful thanks and astonishment at Beatrice's skills, I open the door to find Peter and Jem waiting for me. Jem, rushing to my side, offers his arm and guides me through the hall to the chamber next to the Buttery. I can see that Peter is content to let Jem lead the way.

Before we reach the chamber, I can hear the happy voices within. It feels so good to be safe. Pausing at the door, I take in the scene before me. Morris is waving his arms around and, from what I can gather, is telling an exaggerated tale. Alard, Davy and Owain are looking at Morris with a certain amount of amusement, while Sir William looks confused. Ned is languishing by the fire, his cheeks red from too much ale. To my great joy, Charlemain has rejoined us and is looking well rested.

As I enter, they stand to greet me. Sir William, who is standing by the window, immediately calls out to Young Will. "Will, we are ready. Please can you ask Cook Edgar to serve now?"

Taking my seat by the fire, I sit next to Charlemain. "Oh Charlemain, how I wish that Pip was here to see my beautiful new gown."

With a knowing smile, Charlemain pats my hand and agrees that he, too, wishes that Pip was here to see it.

Once the refreshments have been eaten and everything cleared away, young Will carefully proceeds around the room with a steaming hot bowl of water and fresh linen towels, so that we can all wash our hands. I can now understand why Sir William wanted me to be measured before eating. The beef was delicious and moist, with a sticky honey and herb glaze.

Standing, Sir William announces that he is going to retire for the night, but that he will only be down the hall, should he be needed. "Please feel free to wake me should you need me. Will and my retainers sleep at my door and help is always on call."

Sir William and Will leave the room and we are alone once more.

Alard, who has been relaxing in the window seat stands. "Well, I think that it's nearly time for us all to retire for the night, but first we have some urgent business that we must discuss. Peter and Jem, please could you remain outside and guard the door? Just to make sure that we are not overheard by any passing seamstress."

Peter and Jem leave, before closing the heavy door and securing the latch from outside.

Alard begins, "Ah, we are alone at last. Ned, please do sit up straight and listen."

"Alard, my dear, have no fear, I am fully alert."

With this, Alard makes a face and pulls up a stool. "Our plans have changed and I have now received instructions from Pip." At the sound of Pip's name, my heart leaps, but I also sense danger. "The full details of the kidnap plot have been uncovered. We now know that George and Richard were the intended targets, and that Sir Thomas Stanley has positioned men along the entire length of the south coast in readiness for their landing. A price has been put on their heads and certain death awaits them."

I feel myself go faint at the horrific thought of Duke Richard's boys being murdered. Steadying myself, I ask Alard to continue.

"Stanley's plan is to wipe out the Yorkist line in its entirety. First, the young princes, and then the king, but fortunately this plan has been outwitted. However, we must act fast. George and Richard have been smuggled out of the Burgundian court in hessian sacks. They were disguised as part of a consignment of cloth and were carried out to a waiting cart and loaded, alongside sacks of wool and woad. They landed at Castle Rising in Norfolk six days ago." I consider Castle Rising, before Alard speaks once more. "Castle Rising is and has always been true to the Mortimers and the Yorkists. Queen Isabella spent her final years at the castle mourning the loss of Roger Mortimer and the locals took her to their hearts."

I feel my hem for the small sapphire that is attached to my silk points. Deciding that Castle Rising must be a sign of Isabella's presence, I silently vow to myself to wear the sapphire and points as a bracelet. Concealed within the wide sleeves of my new gown, it will go unnoticed.

Owain, unable to remain silent, asks, "So, the boys are safe?"

"Yes, they are safe, and they are closer than you think. They entered the courtyard this evening with the consignment of Coventry blue broadcloth for Mistress Bethany's gown and the baldricks." Rubbing his head, Alard says, "It was really quite spooky how you mentioned a new gown, Mistress, when you did, but it gave us the cover that we needed."

A shiver runs through my spine. "Yes, very spooky."

Alard continues, "Ned, I am impressed by your quick thinking today. The distraction caused by your awful jester outfit was really quite spectacular."

"Ah well, Alard, I am spectacular in so many ways."

A quiet laughter ripples around the room.

"With all the comings and goings, the boys were carried in by Peter to Sir William's chamber without even being seen. The seamstresses were so hard at work sewing, cutting fabric and discussing Ned's appearance that they never even looked up. Will Catesby has been keeping them company on and off all evening and they are guarded by Sir William's closest confidents at all times. Going forward, they will no longer travel in hessian sacks. They will be dressed in the same blue woollen cloth as the rest of the retinue. Luckily, they are both of a similar size and shape to Jem and Will, so asking for two more sets of hose and tunics did not appear strange to Beatrice. To continue the deception, the entire retinue will be directed to travel with their hoods drawn up at all times. Then, no one who sees us will suspect a thing. We will appear to others as, merely, a fashionable retinue. I have heard that the Beauchamps of Warwick often travel as such nowadays. Will Catesby will also accompany us to Warwick Castle, so there will now be four young pages, rather than one. This will also add to our fashionable status."

Morris is the first to break the stunned silence. "Well, I never, God be praised, but what of Pip?"

"Well, Pip has overseen the first part of the plan and has now left to carry out the second part."

Morris nods. "Can we ask about the second part or is that still a secret?"

"Pip has requested that I tell you all and has given specific instructions for Mistress Bethany." Sitting bolt upright, I listen intently. "The plan is to arrest Lady Stanley and her children. Once arrested, they will be paraded through the streets, before being taken as prisoners to the dungeons of Nottingham Castle, where they will be held until evidence is gathered and a trial is organised. The very sight of Lady Stanley and the children being taken away will immediately spread to Sir Thomas and he will be so consumed with rage that he will follow them with his entire retinue. Then, the king's men will surround Sir Thomas and his retinue just outside of Nottingham. Stanley and his top advisors will be arrested on a charge of planning to kidnap the king's brothers and Lady Stanley will be arrested on a charge of necromancy. Then ,the rest of his retinue will be ordered to disperse and return to their manors immediately, or face imprisonment themselves. This will buy us some time. Sir Thomas is aware of the dungeons at Nottingham Castle, and he knows that once inside he may have lost his wife and heirs forever."

"Will they be executed?"

"No, Mistress, they will just be imprisoned and if they are found to be innocent of any offences, King Edward will pardon them after his coronation and place them under the care of a Yorkist household, where they can do no harm."

"What of Sir Thomas?"

"Ah well, that's another matter entirely. He will be tried along with his supporters, and who knows what their punishment will be. It will all depend on the evidence."

Thinking long and hard, I hesitantly say, "Necromancy?"

"Yes, Mistress, necromancy. It's a terrible thing and punishable by burning, so no stone must be left unturned when gathering evidence, and to this end, Pip has asked that upon arrival at Warwick Castle, you become friends with Lady Stanley. Ingratiate yourself with her. Spend lots of time together and gain her trust. You may just be able to get her to lower her guard."

"Alard, has Lady Stanley has been accused of sorcery before?"

"Yes, but she is sly and calculating, and Sir Thomas has always managed to bully any accusers into staying silent."

With so many questions racing around my head, I think before speaking. "Alard, has anyone at Warwick Castle ever met George and Richard before?"

"Yes, Mistress – Richard, Earl of Warwick, and his wife, Countess Anne. Hence, we need to ensure that the boys are hooded at all times and that they do not cross their paths. On arrival, Peter will take them to your chamber, and they will remain there until King Edward sends orders to the contrary. Jem will also remain in your chamber. They will be well protected. This does mean, however, that you will be sharing a chamber with four others, but please do not worry, all of the beds in the high-status chambers have heavy curtains, which can be drawn for privacy."

"Surely, it will arouse suspicions if three of my pages remain in my chamber?"

"Oh no, this is very common practice nowadays. Pages often remain in the chamber with valuable items and their teacher."

Nervous at the thought of concealing George and Richard's true identity in Warwick's own castle, I take a mouthful of my red wine and stare into the fire.

Alard stands, before inviting us to retire. "We have a

challenging day ahead of us tomorrow. Perhaps we should all retire now and rest. I will introduce George and Richard to you all in the morning, but, for now, I have instructed that they rest. They have suffered greatly over the past four months. First, from the deaths of their father and brother. Then, the deaths of their favourite uncle and cousins, before leaving their mother and residing at the Burgundian Court, before a horrendous journey back to England and across country to Coventry. They are quite naturally scared, although I think that George is rather more robust and will bounce back a little quicker than Richard, by the sounds of things. George appears to be a little louder than Richard, who is meek and quiet."

Retiring for the night, I am escorted back to my chamber by Jem and Peter. Once inside, I sit slumped on the edge of my bed. I have little thought for my surroundings. All I can think of is George and Richard in the chamber next door to me. I long to see their faces and I wonder how much they will resemble Duke Richard. I just cannot imagine the trauma of what they have been through. Losing my mother was the most awful experience in my life and she died naturally. To have your family murdered is another thing entirely. As I undress, I wow to keep them safe and to investigate Lady Stanley thoroughly. It will not be pleasant befriending Lady Stanley, but it must be dome. I will use flattery and cunning to find the answers.

Finally, I kneel by my bedside and grasp a small wooden cross in my clasped hands. *Lord, please help me* are the only words that I can find tonight. My mind is entirely blank. A mixture of shock and sadness. Climbing into the cool linen sheets, I fall asleep immediately.

Thoughts of Kenilworth Castle, Queen Isabella and Roger Mortimer

Waking early, I walk over to a small table by the window, pour some cold water from the jug into a large green-glazed bowl, before proceeding to splash cold water onto my face. My skin begins to tingle and my mind begins to race. Returning to the bed, I sit and contemplate how to ingratiate myself with Lady Stanley. Surely I do not want to seem too keen, as this may alert her suspicions, but if I seem cool and aloof, I may never get close to her. I wonder what she looks like and how she speaks. Does she like playing or listening to music? Or does she prefer being read to? Maybe she likes to play games? Who knows, and what of the others? Are they merely polite travelling companions or are they friends? Do they share the same allegiances? Or do they dislike her? These are the questions that I must find the answers to.

I am woken from my thoughts by a quiet knock on my door and Jem calling out, "Mistress Bethany, I have a jug of hot water for you."

I open the door to find a beaming Jem standing proud and upright in his new blue woollen tunic and white hose. "My, oh my, Jem, Pip will be so proud of you."

Jem beams from ear to ear. "Morris was right; Ned has bought us all new shoes, too. Look." At this, Jem starts to balance precariously on one foot, while raising his other and holding the jug steady.

I laugh and marvel at his balance. "Jem, with a balancing act like that, you will soon be joining Ned as a jester."

Jem, overjoyed at this, begins to dance a merry jig on the spot without spilling a drop of water, before handing me the jug and dancing away.

After washing, I wrap myself in my cloak and sit on the edge of the bed and wait for Beatrice to arrive with my new gown. I am both excited and nervous. Fortunately, I do not have to wait for too long. This time, the door is opened from outside.

"Mistress Bethany, your gown has arrived."

"Thank you, Peter, please show Beatrice in."

With this, Beatrice and two younger seamstresses enter. In their arms is the most beautiful gown that I have ever seen. I now realise that the blue woollen cloth is of a much finer quality than Jem's tunic. The stitching is almost invisible and fine seed pearls adorn both the neckline, the bodice and the sleeves. While Beatrice and the younger seamstress hold the gown up, the other seamstress covers the floor with a large piece of linen.

"Come on, Isolde, our arms are aching!"

Once the linen is down, Beatrice and Isolde lower my gown to the floor, ready for me to step into.

"Now, Mistress, if you would allow us, we would like to help you change into your new gown and under kirtle."

Happily agreeing, I allow myself to enjoy the process of being dressed. The under kirtle is soft and light, the linen being of a much finer fabric than I am used to. Then, it is time to step into my gown. Beatrice and Isolde take my hands to steady me. Once inside, they lift the gown up and help guide my arms into the sleeves. The sleeves are magnificent, and the addition of hidden weights within the hems allows the fabric to move majestically. I long to be alone and to swirl around my room. Lastly, the bodice is threaded with newly woven blue and gold silk laces.

Stepping back, Beatrice looks me up and down, before gently turning me around. Finally, she smiles with satisfaction. "You look a sight to behold, Lady Harsyck, but are you comfortable?"

"Oh yes, Beatrice. It's absolutely gorgeous and it fits like a glove."

"Well, I've done my job then. Let's finish you off." Beatrice asks me to sit down on a stool, which Isolde has just placed in the middle of the room. "I just need to fit your coif and secure it with a few pins." Once fitted, Beatrice requests that Isolde unwraps my new shoes and places them on my feet. Carefully, Isolde does as she is told.

On unwrapping them, I am astounded by the thinness of the sole and the beautiful strap, which is also lined with seed pearls.

"Oh yes, you look as fine as the Duchess Cecily now. The shoes, although impractical, befits your status."

I stand and step carefully around the room, being careful not to slip.

Beatrice, with a look of concern, asks me to stop, before instructing Isolde to rough up the leather soles with the use of a small wire brush. "Isolde, please could you get that shoe brush and gently rub the soles over the ball of each foot? That should prevent Mistress from sliding."

To my surprise, this small adjustment works a treat and I am able to move about without fear. Once complete, Beatrice and her seamstresses bid me a good day and leave.

Within moments, there is another knock at the door. This time, it is Alard. On entering, he bows low in admiration, before we sit in front of the dying fire.

I ask, "Are the boys well?"

"Yes, they passed a good night and they have eaten. George and Richard are practising their sword-fighting skills, with their new wooden swords that Morris carved out for them, while Richard is content to sit and talk with Will. Richard has opened up enough to let us know that he likes to be called Dickon, as that was his father's name for him."

Relief floods over me. "Are they wearing their new clothes?"

"Yes, and they both look splendid. We will certainly be a sight to behold when we enter Warwick Castle. All of Sir Allen's and Sir William's men have also been provided with new hose, new linen shirts and baldricks, but I doubt that they are wearing them yet, as they are dismantling the encampment. We will leave soon, though."

Rising and going over to the window, I survey the dismantling. "Is Warwick very far?"

"No, not very far at all. We will leave via the Greyfriars Gate and travel to Kenilworth Castle via Gibbet Hill."

"Alard, I have heard a little of Kenilworth Castle, but please could you tell me more?"

"Yes, of course. However, I have only ever visited once and it's not a place that I would ever like to visit again. Nowadays, it is a cold and disturbing place, but I hear that it was once a beautiful castle. Many years ago, when Kenilworth was first built, people used to comment on its beauty and how it appeared to float on water. This illusion was caused by a very complex water management system, which drew water from both the Great Mere and the Lower Pool. This water system made the castle one of the most important in the land. Over the years, it has been greatly added to. King Heny V, not content with the complex of castle buildings, gave orders that a pleasance be built within the marshland just outside of the castle. Once complete, it was to be used as both a private hideaway and a grand banqueting venue. In essence, it was to be a castle within a castle. A place of privacy. Set just beyond the sights of the castle and surrounded by two diamond-shaped moats. At one point, it even had its own private dock. A place to entertain and showcase Henry's authority to his very closest companions and visitors. I hear that it was constructed of mainly timber and stone, and that it had four towers."

"You say 'had'. Does that mean that the pleasance no longer exists?"

"Yes, that's correct. Nowadays, most of the timber and stone from the pleasance has been robbed out by the locals and reused to extend their homes and warehouses. You see, the majority of locals in this area are highly militant and, throughout the impositions laid down by the Lancastrian regime, they have remained loyal to the late Queen Isabella, Roger Mortimer and their bloodlines. On the whole staunchly Yorkist, they have been made to suffer, in one way or another, for many years. In this area, stories are still recounted about the glory days of the castle, when

Queen Isabella and Roger Mortimer fell in love and ruled the entire land from Kenilworth. Also about the completion of the Mortimer Tower in honour of the people's favourite, and the time when over one hundred knights descended upon the castle for three days of feasting and jousting in the magnificent tiltyard. Generations have passed down tales of a 'Round Table' similar to the one mentioned in Arthurian legend and joyful times of freedom and stability. However, in recent years, there has been a very dark side to the castle. Queen Margaret, having taken control of it a few years ago, has sought to use the castle as a pawn to further her own ambitions. Its central location is key to her plans. Five years ago, she installed King Henry in the castle. Some say that this was due to Henry's fragile state of mind, whereas others say that King Henry is kept a virtual prisoner by Queen Margaret."

"Alard, is Henry still in residence?"

"No, he has been liberated from the remaining Lancastrian sympathisers and has been removed under King Edward's orders. Henry, although no longer king, will be housed with the greatest respect and care. He will want for nothing, and he is now free to read his many devotional books and spend his days in Godly contemplation."

Unable to stop myself, I picture Queen Margaret and her son, Edward of Lancaster, fleeing to Wales and leaving Henry alone and confused. In an attempt to divert my thoughts, I ask if we will be stopping on our way to Warwick Castle.

"Oh yes, we will break our journey at Kenilworth Abbey. Davy has gone on ahead of us and refreshments will be made available. Davy wanted to check the route for possible traps, and I am glad to say that he has sent word that none were found. It would seem that all of Margaret's men have followed her into Wales."

I stop for a while and consider Wales. From what I have heard, it is a place of great beauty and I wonder if I will ever go there.

Leaving Coventry Behind

A gentle knock on the open door indicates that the time has come to leave. I look over and catch my first sight of George and Dickon, who are standing either side of Sir William. Even without a word being spoken, it is easy to work out who is who. George, standing to the left of Sir William, is taller and more robust-looking. He has the look of his brother, King Edward, whereas Dickon is the image of his father. Slight of frame and delicate, he has a mop of unruly blond hair, which escapes his coif.

Stepping forward, Alard bows and introduces me. "This is Lady Bethany Harsyck."

George looks up for a fleeting second and smiles, but is obviously more interested in his wooden sword. He is turning it this way and that. "Lady Harsyck, I hear that Lord Harsyck is one of the bravest men in the land. Is that true?"

Smiling, I answer yes and think to myself, *He is also the most handsome.*

George, content with the answer, turns to Jem. "Have you met Lord Harsyck?"

A rather startled Jem shakes his head before George begins to fiddle with the leather sheath at his hip.

Addressing Dickon directly, Alard bows once more. Dickon, rather surprisingly, offers up his hand and shakes Alard's, before turning to me and bowing. "Lady Harsyck, I have heard so much about you."

Tears fill my eyes, as Dickon launches himself into me and begins to cry. George, hearing the commotion, stops and looks at his brother. "Dickon, you are wet. What would our father think if he saw you crying."

Dickon holds out his hand and grasps mine. "He would think that I have good manners and that you are rude."

Sir William, keen to keep the peace, steps between the boys and changes the subject. "Now, Lady Harsyck, if you would come with me, I have a present for King Edward that I would like you to deliver to him personally."

Grateful for the cessation of the boys' hostilities, we follow Sir William along the hall, down the spiral staircase and back into the great hall. In the middle of the room sits a large wooden trunk. As we approach, I can see the most glorious stained-glass roundel. It depicts a glorious king, sitting upon a golden throne. The king resembles Edward in nearly all respects.

"This is one of Coventry's most-treasured possessions, and we give it wholeheartedly to King Edward," says Sir William. "It was created by John Thornton at exactly the same time that he created the East Window of York Minster and our very own Guildhall. The reasoning behind our gift is the glorious sun depicted in the top left-hand corner. Edward is our sun. He shines brightly and eclipses all others."

Touched at such a thoughtful gift, I promise to keep the roundel safe and to deliver it myself to the king. With the raising of his right hand, two men approach the table, before placing more straw into the wooden trunk and sealing it carefully.

Outside, Dickon and I climb aboard the cart, with the help of Morris and Charlemain. We make ourselves comfortable, before Morris reminds Dickon to keep his hood drawn up at all times. A smiling Dickon nods and pulls up his hood, before grasping my hand once more.

George, on the other hand, begins to play up. "I don't want to travel in the same cart as my soppy brother. I want to walk with the others."

A smiling Ned approaches. "So, you want to walk with us, do you?" George nods. "Well, that can be arranged, but only if you promise to walk with Owain at all times and to keep your hood drawn up."

George agrees and we set off at a snail's pace in the direction of Kenilworth Priory. Turning around, I wave at Sir William and Prior Gosforth, grateful to both for their kindness.

As I survey my personal retinue, I realise that the addition of new clothes serves two purposes. One, we look splendid and two, there is very little chance of any intruders sneaking into our ranks. Stealing a baldrick would, no doubt, be easy, but stealing someone's hose and boots would be almost impossible. Relaxing slightly, I allow myself to enjoy the bright and sunny day. The time passes quickly and, to my great joy, Dickon has now moved and is sitting next to Charlemain. They are chatting merrily and he appears a little more confident in himself. To my surprise, George has also kept his promise and is walking with Owain. From this distance, I have no idea of their conversation, but if my past experience is anything to go by, Owain is pointing out the sights. I return my attention to myself and the small sapphire, which sits concealed within the fashionable sleeves of my gown.

The quiet of the day is soon shattered as we enter Kenilworth through the Leicester Gatehouse and Morris announces that we are nearing the priory. "Look over there, Mistress. There lies the priory."

Looking up, I gaze upon the walled priory to my left and Kenilworth Castle to my right. The priory is dwarfed by the multitude of castle towers. Morris, full of enthusiasm, proceeds to call out the names of all the towers. "Now we have the Swan Tower, the Lunn's Tower, the Water Tower, the Oriel Tower and, most importantly, the Mortimer Tower. That's the one that dwarfs all of the others."

Dickon, looking up, gasps in delight. True to Alard's word, the castle appears to float on water. As we approach the priory gates, Liege and Freemantle halt of their own accord.

Turning to Dickon, Morris gently asks, "Come on, lad, why don't you take the reins and lead us in?"

Looking around, Dickon notes that both myself and Charlemain are happy for him to move, so – with one quick leap – he takes up his seat next to Morris. On noticing this, George appears jealous and his eyes narrow in annoyance. Slightly alarmed at his demeanour, I determine to keep a close eye on George.

Inside the priory, we are joined by an old friend. Brother Thomas, who, having left Standon, is now residing at Kenilworth. Smiling up at me, he extends his chubby hand and smiles enthusiastically. I notice that his face is as rosy as ever and that he still ties his brown robe with a piece of rope instead of a belt. My heart leaps at the sight of him. Taking his hand, I climb down and embrace him. Standing there holding him, I remember our first meeting and his kindness. I also remember arriving at Standon soaking wet and sitting with everyone by the hearth. I begin to laugh as I recall Ursula removing her coif and proudly displaying her bald head before commenting, "Well, at least I don't have to dry my hair." Those were such happy days!

Once inside, everyone crams into the hall and prepares to break their fast.

I turn to Owain. "Oh no, surely it's not the same feast as at Standon, is it?"

"On yes, Mistress, I can certainly smell the essence of salt fish pottage and nettle soup in the air."

We both laugh at past memories.

Even though I am hungry, I decide not to break my fast and instead I take a seat next to Brother Thomas. "Brother, you are a long way from Standon. What brings you here?"

"Ah, well, that's a very long story. In essence, King Edward wanted his most-trusted followers to relocate to Kenilworth. Our role is to keep our wits about us and note any suspicious comings and goings. Father Bramble is here, too, and he's looking forward to seeing you."

I pat Brother Thomas's chubby hand and notice how his silver hair glints in the firelight.

Looking over towards Owain, I notice that George has kept true to his promise and is eating by Owain's side. Perhaps I am wrong; perhaps he is an inherently good boy who just appears jealous or perhaps he's just dealing with his loss in a more robust manner than Dickon. I just don't know. Turning my attention back to Davy, Ned, Alard, Peter and Charlemain,

I note that they all have their boots off and are resting by the fire, while Jem, Will and Dickon are sitting quietly by the fire. My heart is warmed by Jem's attention to detail, for he is performing his page duties with great diligence.

Sitting silently next to Brother Thomas, I look into the flames and consider the task that lies ahead of me, until Father Bramble arrives. Standing, we also embrace as old friends. Only now do I realise that they all knew of my lineage and took great care to shelter me and protect me on my way to Walsingham. Sitting slightly apart from the others, I ask if they have seen anything that I should be aware of.

The brothers look at one another before Thomas speaks, "Yes and no. There have been a great deal of comings and goings up at the castle in the last few days, but no more than I would expect, as I hear that everyone is making their way to Warwick Castle to travel onwards to London together. However, Lady Stanley arrived yesterday, just before nightfall, and God forgive me for saying this, but I really don't like her. She appears sly and guarded and I was disturbed to see that her men had changed out of their usual livery – instead of displaying the full Stanley coat of arms, they are using the full arms of the King of Mann. To my mind, this spells trouble as there can only be one king in this realm."

"Brother Thomas, please can you describe a little of the history of the King of Mann to me?"

"Yes, of course, my dear. The title of King of Mann is an ancient title. So ancient that it goes back to the early Norse rulers and Godred Crovan, the King of Dublin and the Isles. Henry IV, a spiteful and cruel man, seized the title from William le Scrope. Yes, I see from your eyes that you recognise the name. William was first cousin to Archbishop

Richard Scrope." We cross ourselves before carrying on. "As well as seizing the title, he seized all of the King of Mann possessions. The Isle, the Peel and the Lordship. The Peel being the castle. He took this action as he was vengeful against Henry Percy, the Earl of Northumberland. He sought to rid the land of anyone who supported King Richard II and, to this end, Archbishop Scrope was also executed for his support of the Percy family. Henry IV was a wicked, wicked man. Then he granted the tenure of the Isle on Mann to one of his greatest supporters, Sir John Stanley, from where the title and rights have been handed down to Sir Thomas Stanley. So, you see, the Stanleys have an over-mighty view of themselves and their status. I wouldn't be at all surprised if the use of the Arms of Mann wasn't a call to Lancastrians to overthrow King Edward. The colour of their livery is blood red background with a three-legged device, the legs of which are clad in silver armour and adorned further with gold detailing."

My mind begins to race, as I consider the words of Father Thomas. What if there is another plot that no one knows of? What if this plot is related to the kidnap plot? I fiddle with my concealed sapphire and consider what to do next.

Standing, I walk over to the window where Morris is standing. Leaning in close, I whisper, "Morris, I am worried. Do you know of Pip's whereabouts or how we can get word to him?"

"As I believe it, Pip has gone ahead of us to Warwick. Why, is there a problem?" Morris frowns.

"Well, to be honest, I don't know. It's something that Father Thomas has just mentioned. Lady Stanley's retinue has changed their livery from that of the Stanleys to the Arms of the King of Mann, and Brother Thomas feels that this could be a sign to all the disaffected Lancastrians to overthrow King Edward."

Morris pats my arm affectionately. "Ah well, Brother Thomas has read my mind. I also noted this as we entered through the Leicester Gatehouse. I saw two men dressed in Mann livery lounging by the wall. They looked shifty and turned their backs on us as we passed. Sir Allen also noted the livery and had a small number of his men leave the retinue to challenge them. It would appear that both of them were Lady Stanley's men and that they were keeping lookout, but we don't know what they were looking out for. Both are now being held in the castle as prisoners. Lady Stanley will no doubt wonder where they have gone when they do not report back to her, but as she cares little about anyone, she will not send scouts to look for them."

Relieved to know that Pip is safe, and that the Stanley lookouts are now prisoners, I return to the group.

Alard is the first to speak. "I hope that you are all rested now, as the time has come to leave. Rather than stay here for the night, I think that it would be wise for us to leave and travel direct to Warwick Castle. I hear that Lady Stanley and her retinue are firmly housed within Kenilworth Castle, and, if we go now, we can get on the road and be ahead of them. Then we will be ensconced in Warwick well before their arrival. It's always better to have the upper hand and this manoeuvre will mean that we are not disadvantaged."

At this, everyone puts their boots back on and rearranges their clothing, ready to depart. Back in the cart, I am joined by Charlemain and Morris. Covering our laps with matching blue woollen throws, Morris quickly shakes the reins and calls out.

On the move again, I am pleased to see that George is still by Owain's side on the left of the cart and Dickon, Will and Jem are walking with Peter on the right. Dickon appears a little more confident in Will and Jem's company and I smile when I see that Dickon has his wooden sword strapped to his side.

As we pass Kenilworth Castle, I marvel at the sight. In the dimming afternoon light, the stone appears to be almost red in colour, with the lowering making patterns on the walls. Looking up at Mortimer Tower, I cannot help but think of Queen Isabella and Roger Mortimer, and their great love for one another. I begin to fiddle with the small sapphire concealed within the sleeve of my gown, before my thoughts turn once more to Warwick and the task at hand.

Warwick Castle. Here We Come.

I'm not entirely sure what I expected Warwick to be like, but I certainly never imagined anything like this. Looking this way and that, I try to take everything in.

Charlemain, aware of my shock, pats my hand. "It's busy today, I give you that."

Morris, keen to join our conversation, calls out, "Yes, it's an absolute nightmare. I'm going to have to rein in Fremantle and Liege to a walking pace and even that may be too fast."

As we slow down, Morris lifts his left hand in a bid to get everyone's attention. Alard and Davy both sprint to Morris's side before Alard asks, "What's up, Morris?"

"Look ahead, lad, look. The north gate. It's completely rammed. There are people everywhere – and is that a queue that I can see, or are my old eyes deceiving me?"

Alard, looking up, immediately seems concerned. "You're not deceived, Morris, but I'm not entirely sure that it's a queue. It looks more like the entire population of Saltisford have come out and are lining the streets."

Morris appears perplexed. "But why? Do you think that they are expecting to see something or someone?"

"I don't know, Morris. Our scouts certainly haven't reported anything back to me, and as Lady Stanley and her retinue are safely ensconced within Kenilworth Castle, they can't be waiting for Lady Stanley."

Charlemain says, "Perhaps they are expecting us? We travel now as the grand retinue of Lord and Lady Harsyck – and, as such, we may be an attraction?"

Alard nods. "Yes, you might be right there, but I suggest that we proceed with caution. Heaven knows who's in that crowd."

Sitting upright, I beckon to Owain, who comes immediately. "Owain, do you think that it would be wise for Dickon and George to travel in the cart with us?"

Before answering, Owain rubs his brow. "Probably not, as it may arouse suspicions. You see, pages never ever travel in the cart along with their master or mistress. They always attend it, but I can see your point. I'll ask the boys to pull their hoods up as far as possible, and then George and Jem will walk in front of me, and Will and Dickon will walk in front of Peter. This way, they'll be in our direct line of sight at all times."

Content with this plan, I nod my head, before Alard instructs Morris and Davy to watch the crowds. Morris shakes the reins and we roll on at an extremely slow pace. As we near the north gate, Morris enthusiastically points out the sights of interest. I can see numerous grand houses and taverns, a hospital, the church of St Michael's and St Sepulchre's Priory. Morris calls out, "We're in the heart of Saltisford now – so called because it is the ending of the salt-way from Droitwich to Warwick. When I was young, this was the most desirable area outside of the walls. Look over there and you will see St Sepulchre's fishponds and the mighty River Avon. I used to swim in the river long ago. It is deep and fast-moving, hence the bridges in this area need constant attention. Not long ago, I heard that the stone bridge to the east of here was being rebuilt yet again, as three of the arches were becoming unstable. The streets around here are a maze and it's very easy to get lost; to our left, we have Bowling Green Street, Theatre Street and Joyce Pool, and to our right, we have Chapel Street, Gerrard Street and Mill Street. It's a grand area."

As we pass, people wave enthusiastically and, in keeping with my position as Lady Harsyck, I smile and wave back.

Relieved to have passed through the gate, I am astounded by the sheer size of Warwick Castle. Sitting high upon a hill, it dominates the entire town. It is magnificent! Even at this distance, I can see a great many windows, numerous towers and battlements that stretch into infinity. Unlike Kenilworth, this stone is light in colour and much more pleasing to the eye. If I'm correct, it is made from a type of sandstone.

Morris, keen to impress everyone with his knowledge, begins once more, "You see over there… the River Avon acts as a formidable moat, and directly in front of us is the heavily fortified barbican and gatehouse. No one can get inside Warwick Castle unless they are invited in, that's for sure. The curtain walls on the town side are just as impenetrable as the deep and treacherous waters of the moat. And then you see that glorious tower standing higher than any of the others? Well, that's known as Guy's Tower. It's named after the 10th Earl of Warwick, Guy de Beauchamp. It has twelve sides and is five storeys high. Archers keep a lookout from the top both day and night. Standing well above the defensive walls, the archers have a clear line of sight and use their arrows on anyone who is foolish enough to try and break the defences. They can also drop boiling hot oil or heavy stones onto people from the holes of the parapet. Guy's Tower houses the highest status rooms anywhere in the castle and, as such, they are the best defended."

Turning his attentions back to Fremantle and Liege, Morris skilfully asks both horses to climb the hill, while keeping our cart in a straight line. As we approach, the spiked iron defences are raised and the mighty gates of the barbican are opened for us to enter. Inside, I see a multitude of tents to the left and open gardens to our right. The tents are white and gold and emblazoned with the diagonal red cross of the Nevilles.

Charlemain, leaning in close, says, "That is the encampment of Maud Stanhope, Lady Willougby, the widow of Thomas Neville."

On hearing Thomas's name, my heart sinks, as I know that Thomas was killed at the Battle of Wakefield and that his head was impaled on a spike next to Duke Richard's on Micklegate Bar in York.

"I believe that we will meet Lady Willougby tonight when we eat in the great hall."

I nod in silent recognition, unable to speak due to a lump in my throat.

Ahead of us, a young page – similar in age to Jem – is directing our retinue to the gardens on the right. "Over here, Master. This is where your retinue will set up camp. We have left a store of logs by the wall, along with barrels of water for your ease."

Alard, impressed by the young page's attention to detail, thanks him. Looking around, I spy Ned lounging against a wooden rail. He is playing his shawm, while the retinue of Lady Willoughby stamp and clap in time to the rhythm. I wondered where Ned had got to!

Climbing down from the cart, I take Charlemain's arm and prepare to leave the others. Concerned for the safety of Dickon and George, I bid them a very fond farewell for now, as they must remain within the encampment with the rest of the retinue. To Alard's delight, Ned has stopped playing his shawm and now joins us.

"Do not fear, Bethany, both Sir Allen's and Sir William's men will form a protective barrier around the boys. They will be safer out here with us than inside, where they run the risk of their aunts and uncles recognising them."

I turn and walk in the direction of the entrance. Stopping at the threshold, I smooth the wool of my kirtle, straighten my coif and rearrange my cloak. Ned enters first, then Owain, Charlemain and myself. Inside the great hall, my eyes are immediately drawn to the dais where Anne Beauchamp, the Countess of Warwick, is sitting, surrounded by her daughters. Demure and confident, the countess stands and prepares to receive us into her home.

"Welcome, you must be Lady Bethany Harsyck."

I curtsy before responding, "Yes, Countess. I am Bethany Harsyck."

"Well, you're very welcome. I take it that your retinue has been shown to the area that has been prepared for them?"

"Oh yes. Thank you, Countess – they are well provided for."

"I instructed that they be placed next to Lady Willoughby's retinue on the higher ground of the inner bailey. I have saved the lower area, which is inclined to be damp and marshy, for Lady Stanley's men." Sensing a slight smile cross her lips, I lower my eyes. "I have never much liked my sister-in-law and I only tolerate her for my husband's sake."

I sense that the Countess of Warwick is playful, but I fear her boldness.

"Please let me introduce our daughters. This is Isobel, and Anne, and Margaret."

At this, all three girls rise and curtsy to me. It is immediately obvious who Margaret is. In comparison to Isobel and Anne, Margaret is tall and sturdy. She has darker features and sparkling green eyes. Isobel and Anne are slight of build and have their mother's fair complexion.

Realising that I have not introduced our party, I say, "Countess, I would like you to meet my private advisers and dearest companions – Charlemain Harsyck, Ned Harsyck and Owain de Acre."

In turn, all three bow to the countess, before bowing to her daughters. Immediately, I note that Margaret is really quite smitten by Ned.

Seemingly unaware, the countess continues, "As it is late, I suggest that we eat now and that you are shown to your chambers later. Does that please you?"

"Oh yes. Thank you, Countess."

The countess beckons over a page. "Timkin, please escort Lady Harsyck and her companions to their places." I curtsy once more before walking away from the dais.

Taking our seats at the top of the right-hand table, I position myself so that I can survey the entire great hall. Directly opposite us, I can see an extremely slim lady dressed entirely in black, with a veil covering her face. Realising this to be Lady Willoughby, my heart sinks in pity and sadness for it is obvious that she is deep in mourning. She is surrounded by her ladies in waiting, who fuss her constantly, although I doubt that she even sees them, for her eyes are cold and unseeing.

Charlemain gently nudges me. "That is, indeed, Lady Willoughby, and to the left of her retinue sits Countess Elizabeth Butler, the widow of John Talbot, the second Earl of Shrewsbury and Waterford. Be especially careful of her, Bethany. She is danger. John Talbot was cut down by Duke Richard when he was found by King Henry's tent at the Battle of Northampton. He was a traitor, and we suspect that she is also a traitor. She travels with her eight children and I hear that she seeks advantageous betrothals for each of them. Sadly, though, her youngest daughter, Margaret, who was born last year, died soon after. No one really knows what happened, but the shock of her husband dying may have caused the death."

I allow a little sadness to fill my heart for Elizabeth, as to lose a child must be devastating, but I do not dwell on the issue. "You say Butler – is this the same branch as Lady Eleanor Talbot, also known as Butler?"

"Yes, Bethany."

As I take all of this information in, I have little interest in the food that is being brought to the table, although it smells delicious. The countess has provided a most substantial meal. Before me, there is a platter of cooked meats, which is decorated with flavoured jellies. I suspect that the green jelly has been prepared with wild garlic and the yellow jelly has been prepared with saffron. There are loaves of fine white pandemain bread and pats of golden butter before me. I note that the butter has been enriched with sea salt. I know it to be sea salt due to the slightly brownish colour and the way that the crystals cling to the butter.

As I eat, I continue to survey the great hall. It is oddly quiet with very few people talking to one another, although this is not surprising as I can feel an immense amount of tension in the air. I suspect that the tension will grow even further when Lady Stanley and her children arrive.

The Arrival of Lady Stanley

The morning breaks in spectacular style. I rise from my bed and walk over to the window to witness the worsening weather. The sky is ashen and a particularly violent thunderstorm is rumbling all around. Bolts of lightning explode from heavy grey clouds and the rain lashes down. From my apartment in Guy's Tower, I look down upon the ever-growing encampment and feel immense gratitude to Countess Anne for giving our retinue the higher ground. Alard made the right call to travel yesterday, as today the roads will be slippery and the mud deep. This way, everyone will have cover – be it under waxed linen canopies or within the fine stone stables. I wonder where the boys are and pray that they are safe.

Dressing quickly, I prepare myself for the day ahead. In truth, I have little on my mind except for befriending Lady Willoughby. I expect this to be nigh on impossible, but I must try.

Downstairs in the great hall once more, I break my fast with Charlemain, Owain and Ned, before approaching Lady Willoughby, who now sits alone.

"Good morrow, Lady Willoughby, may I sit with you?"

Expecting to be pushed away, I am surprised when Lady Willoughby invites me to take the stool next to her. "Yes. I am sorely in need of company today."

I smile and take a seat. Even through Lady Willoughby's black lace veil, I can see her red and swollen eyes.

"Please forgive me, I am not in my right mind. I am Maud Stanhope, Lady Willoughby, widow of Sir Thomas Neville, but I expect that you know all of that." As the words leave her lips, she begins to sob violently.

Not knowing what to do for the best, I allow Lady Willoughby time to regain her composure.

"I believe that you are Lady Harsyck, previously Bethany Mortimer – am I correct?"

"Yes."

"Well, I am very pleased to meet you at last, Bethany, but how I wish that we had met under better circumstances. A few years ago, Richard, Duke of York spoke about you and your loyalty to our branch of the family. He spoke about your husband, too – Lord Phillip Harsyck, a brave and loyal retainer. Now, I only have memories of the family that your husband once defended. My husband lies dead and headless in Pontefract Castle with my father-in-law, his uncle and many others. I grieve not only because of their deaths, but because I am unable to visit them and pour my tears onto their broken bodies. My ladies in waiting are fools; they think that they can cheer me up by reading poetry and playing the harp. They are mad. The words of Chaucer that my husband and I once read together are shrill and meaningless upon their lips. The only joy that I have in my life is the knowledge that Edward will soon sit on the throne of England and be officially crowned as King of England. Edward sent word to me a few days ago. He has invited me to stay at Windsor Castle indefinitely. He wishes me to be safe and well maintained, and far away from any potential suitors who may seek to marry me. I am eternally grateful to Edward as I have no desire to ever marry again. I may even become a nun and be wedded to our Lord. Who knows?"

We sit in a comfortable silence, content and understanding of each other's grief. Raising her pale hand, Lady Willoughby asks me to move closer.

"You must go now, Bethany. My ladies are returning and I do not wish you to be subjected to their idiocies – but beware, I must tell you of a plot that I have heard of. Lady Stanley's husband, Sir Thomas, has fled to the south coast to abduct Edward's younger brothers, Dickon and George, and Lady Stanley is due to arrive here later this morning. She now fashions herself as the Queen of Mann. She is evil. Please do not be drawn into her web of deceit. She acts as a friend and then she stings anyone who gets close to her." Lady Willoughby grasps my hand and smiles, before I leave her.

Sitting once more to the left of the dais, I can hear Anne, the Countess of Warwick, singing sweetly to her daughters. Her face is full of love and kindness.

Realising that I now sit alone, she beckons me to her side. "I see that your retainers have left you all alone. Please join me and the girls. We are always pleased to have company. This castle, although grand, is not as homely as Middleham where we live. At Middleham, we are free to explore. The evils of the world are largely unknown to us. We walk in the hills, fish in the rivers and ride our horses over to Morpeth. We sing and dance joyfully. Middleham is just too beautiful for words! The air is clean, and I can sense the spirits of my of mother and father-in-law when I am there. Whereas Warwick is a building site, with people rushing this way and that at all hours. You must have heard the terrible din outside. The silence is broken by banging and shouting, and that is mainly in part to my father's will and my husband, Richard, Earl of Warwick, who you will meet later. Richard is having at least twenty houses constructed, the dean's house rebuilt, the churchyard boundaries moved, and the Lady Chapel, often referred to as the Beauchamp Chapel, within St Mary's Church, completely renovated. This church has been the final resting place of my family for nearly one hundred years and after my father died in Rouen in April 1439, work began on extending the Lady Chapel to accommodate his tomb. In keeping with his status as King Henry VI's tutor and a trusted general for many years, his tomb will take centre stage in the enlarged chapel, as it is expected that people will travel from far and wide to pay their respects. I hear that it will be elaboratively decorated and on it will lie a life-size bronze statue of my father in full armour. His sleeping body lying on a funeral bier. I have been told that William Austen of London is creating the statue and has already started to prepare the moulds for it. Lower down the tomb, there will be small niches, which will eventually hold bronze statues of us, his family, when we pass over."

I notice that the Countess begins to shudder, before continuing, "I am told that the Beauchamp Chapel will be magnificent when it is finished and the windows will house beautiful stained glass, emblazoned with the coat of arms of the de Beauchamp family. Oh, such beauty. Set against a backdrop of red, there will be a central golden banner with three golden crosses above and three golden crosses below."

Quick to change the subject from her father, the countess moves onto the building work in general. "I believe that Richard employs over one hundred masons at present and that he is seeking even more. The buildings in the college are also being renovated and reconstructed. Warwick will be the feather in my husband's cap when finished and one of the mightiest towns in the land. However, I doubt that I will ever see the culmination of his work, as we plan on returning to Middleham after the coronation, and once there, I will not leave again, unless Edward marries."

Considering this, I wonder if she speaks of anyone in particular or is just ruminating on future events. Is it immediately obvious that the countess wishes to forget the sadness of her father's death and that she wishes to concentrate on her three daughters, who are now walking up and down the great hall, practising how to walk demurely in preparation for Edward's coronation. Anne, obviously frustrated, tries but fails over and over again to stand, walk, stop, curtsy and then stand again, without wobbling from back to front and losing her balance. Trying not to chuckle at Anne's frustration, we take a seat and encourage all three girls to continue.

The countess explains that Margaret is nearly sixteen, Isobel is ten years of age and Anne is five going on twenty. "Anne's certainly her father's daughter. She likes to be well presented and absolutely loves new shoes and new clothes, whereas Margaret and Isobel are more like me – laid-back and comfortable with being in the background."

I suspect that Anne will practise for a long time, until she gets it just right.

The day passes in a pleasant haze, and I wonder where Owain, Ned and Charlemain have got to. However, much later, the calmness of the day is completely destroyed by the arrival of Lady Stanley and her retinue. Outside, from within the inner bailey, shouting can be heard.

"No, my men will not set up camp in that marshy ground. Don't you know who I am? Richard, Earl of Warwick, is my brother, and he will be sorely displeased at your treatment of me and my retinue."

Unfortunately, I am unable to make out the response, but as there is no spare room, I imagine that Lady Stanley's retinue has no option but to set up camp in the space that has been made available for them.

With an almighty bang, the door of the great hall opens and Lady Margaret strides in at a pace. Soaked from head to foot, she is bedraggled and angry. Walking over to the dais, she immediately confronts the Countess Anne.

"Where is my brother? I demand to know."

Shaking her head, Anne starts to wobble. Immediately, the girls rush to her side and cling onto their mother. Fearful of their aunt, they shiver.

"Welcome, Eleanor, I am unsure where Richard is at present, but he will be here for tonight's feast. Your chamber is ready for you, if you would like to retire and rest."

"My chamber, my chamber – of course my chamber is ready for me! I am Lady Stanley and you will address me as such at all times. You are nothing to me and I'm only here to see my brother and to take up my rightful place in Edward's coronation."

With this, Lady Stanley turns around and almost knocks over Lady Willoughby. "Get out of my way, you good-for-nothing Yorkist! You and your family have torn this country to pieces, and I wish to have nothing to do with you."

As Lady Stanley leaves the room, with her ladies in waiting following at a pace, it feels like a whirlwind has just blown in, torn everything to pieces and then vanished. I can't say that I relish the thought of meeting Lady Stanley at tonight's feast. In all honesty, I wish that we could arrest her immediately.

Returning to my chamber, accompanied by Owain, Ned and Charlemain, who have just returned from visiting St Mary's church, I wonder if Peter has managed to smuggle Jem, Dickon and George in unseen. As the door is opened, I fear that Peter has been unsuccessful as I can see no sign of life. However, as we all enter and close the door behind us, all four appear from a separate chamber to the side of the mantelpiece. God be praised. Tears begin to roll uncontrollably down my face and I embrace each as a mother would embrace her own children. Looking up, I see a sea of relieved and smiling faces. Peter is the first to break the silence.

"Yes, God be praised, but Lady Stanley, too. If she hadn't caused such a commotion, I doubt that I could have smuggled all three into Guy's Tower unchallenged as the earl's security is extremely tight. However, when Lady Stanley verbally attacked the Countess Anne, the earl's men left their station and rushed to the great hall, fearing the worst. If we had been challenged, I'm certain that the earl's men would have wanted to see our papers, but luckily, all three boys are safe now and they can stay here until any danger has passed. Fortunately, this chamber is the furthest from the rest of the castle guests, so the boys can play, read, write and live unhindered. I have also double-checked and anyone standing at the windows cannot be identified, so we have no fear there either. The door will be guarded at all times, with Alard, myself and Davy taking it in turns. Morris will stay in the stables with Fremantle and Liege, with Sir William and Sir Allen close by, while Ned, Owain and Charlemain will remain with you at all times."

Gratefully, I touch Peter's arm, for he is the best thing to have come out of Pontefract and my awful visit to the castle.

Uncovering a Necromancer

Now that the boys are safely ensconced within my chamber and our retinue is in place, it is time for me to begin my work. At this evening's feast, I have the unenviable task of attempting to befriend Lady Stanley, although I have absolutely no idea of how I am going to do this. She is cold and aggressive, and we have nothing in common, but I have a plan. Changing into my brown cloak and matching coif, I wonder if this will be enough to arouse Lady Stanley's curiosity. She may well wonder why I wear mourning dress, and this may just be enough to tempt her into conversation.

Surprisingly, the seating arrangements have been changed and I now find myself on the top table alongside the Countess Anne and her three daughters, with Lady Stanley to my right. Lady Willoughby and Countess Elizabeth are seated to the Countess Anne's left, to the far side of the vacant seat, which has been prepared for Richard, Earl of Warwick. I do not relish this prospect, but at least I should have the chance to engage in conversation.

Taking my place, I smile and remain silent until the doors are closed, the trumpets sound and Richard, Earl of Warwick strides to the top table. Stopping in front of his wife and daughter, he bows low and winks at the girls, who immediately giggle in unison. Then, without a word of warning, he approaches everyone on the top table in turn, with his valet de chambre by his side, and welcomes everyone.

As Warwick approaches, I am overcome by an unknown smell. It is uplifting and light, yet earthy at the same time. I start to quiver inside as my turn to be introduced grows ever closer.

"Ah… so you are Bethany Mortimer, Lady Harsyck." With these words, Warwick bows to me as I attempt to stand before him. With a wave of his hand, he quickly indicates that he would like me to remain seated. "Please do not stand; there is no need. I feel like I already know you, even though we missed each other at Towton Hall. I arrived a little too late that day and was ensconced with King Edward for far too long, and when we emerged, you had gone. However, Lord Harsyck, your husband, remained and I spoke to him at length about the recent events, and my father and brother in particular. It was that dreadful day that my men travelled to Micklegate to reclaim the heads of our loved ones. I can see from your attire that you still mourn."

Nodding and smiling, I am stunned into silence and wonder what he actually knows, or rather what he would wish me to believe that he knows.

Moving onto Lady Stanley, he greets his sister warmly, "Oh Eleanor, my cherished sister, how are you?"

Leaning forward and whispering, Eleanor begins, "Well, Richard, things could be better. That bitch of a wife of yours has ordered that my retinue be housed on the marshy land within the inner bailey. She has given me a single chamber with no room for my ladies in waiting; my children and their nannies are on the other side of the castle; and then, worst of all, when I arrived, she dishonoured me in front of everyone."

Knowing this to be a lie, I have to contain myself and keep my true feelings hidden.

With a soft appeasing voice, Warwick replies, "Eleanor, my dear, please forgive me, for if I had been here, this would not have happened. Please leave this with me and I will reprimand Anne for her behaviour." Then, with a kiss on Eleanor's cheek, he walks behind the table and takes his seat. Never before have I felt so uncomfortable, but at least Eleanor lowered her guard in front of me.

Unable to eat, I merely look at the dishes before me as sickness wells up in the pit of my stomach, whereas Lady Stanley obviously has quite an appetite. To my surprise, she has little manners and eats with her fingers – the grease running down her hands to her wrists and then to the hem of her sleeve. Remove after remove are presented and taken away, until I see something that I just cannot resist. A soft runny brie accompanied by savoury fritters. Leaning forward, I attempt to catch the eye of a server, with no success.

To my surprise and embarrassment, Lady Eleanor, noticing my attempts, calls out loudly, "You, server! Come here. We want brie and fritters."

Shocked, the server appears frozen to the spot.

"I said we want brie. Serve us, you oaf."

With this, the great hall goes silent, as a very young boy approaches where we sit. "Please forgive me. I did not mean to ignore you."

"Well, you did, and you'll pay the price, but before you do, I said that we want brie and fritters."

Never before have I seen such fear in a server's eyes. With shaking hands, the young boy carefully scoops up the brie and places it on top of the fritters and bacon, before even more carefully transferring it to our trenchers. Stepping back, he bows and I thank him. Lady Stanley, on the other hand, looks angry.

"How dare you presume that I wanted my food served in this manner! Richard, Richard, dismiss this boy at once."

Standing, Warwick calls the boy over to him and mutters a few unheard words before dismissing the boy, who immediately bows and leaves. I can tell from his stance that he is crying. Now, anger replaces the sick feeling in my stomach.

Lady Stanley, unaware or uncaring of anyone's displeasure with her, breaks the silence and begins talking to me, "How is your brie?"

"It is delicious, thank you."

"Good. I should hate you to be disappointed. Years ago, when my father and brothers lived, we would have magnificent feasts, with only the very best. Now, my brother seeks to keep up this tradition, even though he receives no support from that useless wife of his."

Looking into Lady Stanley's eyes, I can see that she truly hates the Countess Anne. But I soon realise that I should not have worried, as she is more than happy to engage with me, even if it is to blow her own trumpet.

She continues, "My father, who I believe you met, was a magnificent man and well loved by King Henry IV until he fell in with Richard, Duke of York. How I hated that man."

Barely concealing my anger, I can feel myself flush. How dare she dishonour Duke Richard's memory. I immediately want to use my knife, which hangs from my belt, to stab her to death. However, biting my lip and breathing deeply, I regain my composure.

Lady Stanley, on the other hand, begins to scream, "That man! That man! It's his fault entirely that my father and brother lie dead."

Warwick, seemingly annoyed, stands and joins us immediately. "Sister, do not speak such words. They are treasonous and King Edward will be most displeased. You could get us both executed."

"Oh really… that good-for-nothing cousin of ours. I'm not scared of him."

With these words and to my surprise, Sir Allen and Sir William immediately rush towards the top table and seize Lady Stanley by the shoulders. Sir William's face, almost purple with rage, has started to sweat, while Sir Allen's eyes have gone black and his skin white. The great hall buzzes with nervous energy.

With Lady Stanley overpowered, Sir William says, "I, Sir William Herbert, Lord of Pembroke, stand here for our true and loyal king, King Edward IV of England, and I am arresting this woman, Eleanor, Lady Stanley, on a charge of treason and necromancy. She is a traitor and you, my Lord of Warwick, I would tread most carefully if I were you, for instead of arresting Lady Stanley, as is your duty, you seek to pacify her. Have you treachery in your heart, too? For if you have, I will arrest you, too."

Knowing himself to be cornered, Warwick steps back, raises his hands and announces that he has no treachery in his heart and that it is his sister who should be arrested and not him. Shocked at Warwick's self-preservation, I stare at both of them in disbelief.

Sir William continues, "Eleanor, Lady Stanley, you will be taken from this place to your chamber, where your body and belongings will be searched. Lady Harsyck and Lady Willoughby, I would like you both to accompany us, as witnesses to what we find."

I nod in silence, whereas Lady Willoughby is not so quiet. "I will be more than pleased to witness this witch's downfall. My spies have told me that she carries with her carved wooden moulds of our beloved King Edward and his only surviving brothers, George and Richard. I have heard that she fashioned these moulds herself using a chisel and a small knife. Skills that she learnt in Ormskirk, no doubt. I have been led to believe that the one of King Edward is extremely lifelike, whereas the other two are not so. I expect that this is down to the fact that she has spent very little time with King Edward's two much younger brothers – but do not be deceived, she hates them all. She wishes them dead, like my poor husband, but I'll see her lifeless body lying on the ground and covered in blood, and her head on a spike, before that happens."

I bow to Countess Anne before I leave the top table and notice that she is shaking violently. She grasps my arm and pulls me close. No doubt fearful of others overhearing our conversation, she whispers in my ear, "Bethany, before you go, I want you to know that I had also heard of the plot that Lady Maud speaks of. One of my maids was informed by her suitor that he saw Eleanor buying a vast quantity of wax suitable for boiling, in the market, before she arrived."

Smiling and grateful to be trusted, I pat the countess on the shoulder. "Thank you for telling me. I am most grateful."

Once inside Lady Stanley's chamber, Sir William and Sir Allen lock the door before releasing Lady Stanley. Unperturbed, and like a madwoman, Lady Stanley begins to scream hysterically before banging on the door.

"Let me out! Let me out! How dare you imprison me?! You have no right to search either my body or my belongings. I demand that you let me go. My husband will be sorely displeased with you, and I can guarantee that you will suffer if I am not released."

I notice that Sir William, who was once calm, is now close to boiling point. "I have every right as King Edward's man to hold you and search you, and I'm telling you now that if I find objects associated with witchcraft, you will be transported immediately to the dungeons at Nottingham Castle, where you will be held until a trial can be arranged. Your husband would be wise to distance himself from your actions, for if he is also found to be a traitor, you will both be held and if found guilty, executed. Now, I demand that you stop screaming immediately and sit down, for if you do not do so of your own accord, I will have you bound and gagged. My men, who are on guard outside, have heavy chains about their persons and they are longing to use them. I demand that you be quiet."

With this, Lady Stanley takes a step back and falls silent. However, the silence doesn't last for very long. For with black eyes and a look of utter hatred, Lady Stanley lurches straight towards me.

"I hate you, Lady Bethany Harsyck – or should I say, I hate you, Bethany Mortimer. You pauper, you. You're nothing more than a base member of the traitorous Mortimer family. I hate your family and, most importantly, I hate all Yorkists."

Standing shocked, I feel paralysed and unable to defend myself. My head begins to throb. Still unable to move, I'm aware that Lady Stanley has ripped the coif from my head and is now tugging at my hair. I feel faint and blackness descends.

On waking, I find myself in the arms of Owain. The situation reminds me of when I was attacked at Newmarket on my pilgrimage to Walsingham. Owain was by my side then and is by my side once more.

"Bethany, can you hear me?"

Struggling to sit up, I realise that blood is pouring down the side of my face and onto my kirtle. I am stunned. Lady Maud is standing over me, holding a piece of blood-soaked linen in her hand. She is silently sobbing, while trying to stem my blood.

Finding my voice, I ask, "What has happened to me? Why can't I remember?"

To this, a very anxious-looking Peter kneels by my side. "Mistress Bethany, I am so sorry. I have failed you. I should have remained in the room by your side, not outside, where I was no use at all." He shakes his head. "Please forgive me. I will never leave your side again."

Sinking back into Owain's arms, I begin to remember the horror of Lady Stanley's attack. "Where is Lady Stanley? What has happened to her?"

Sir William kneels besides Peter. "She is locked in the chamber next door. I've made sure that she is bound tightly in chains and is gagged. My men guard her, while a cart is being prepared to take her to Nottingham Castle."

"Did you search her belongings?"

"Yes, and what I found confirmed our beliefs. She was

in possession of a great quantity of wax, three wooden moulds, three wax effigies, two small knives, steel pins and a chisel. Luckily, I noticed that Lady Stanley also had a blade concealed within the folds of her sleeves, and I managed to hurl her to the floor before she could cut you. However, I was not quite quick enough and a scuffle ensued. She fought like a wild animal and tore at your ear."

Lifting my hand, I feel for my ear.

Lady Maud, still sobbing, takes my hand. "Please do not worry. Your ear bleeds profusely, but it is not deformed."

Relieved, I am content to hold Maud's hand. Time stands still, but not for long. Still lying upon the floor, I hear the lock turn in the door and the latch open. With so many people, kneeling by my side, I cannot see who has just entered, but I know immediately who it is. A strong sweet smell of mint floats in the air.

Unable to help myself, I call out, "Pip! Pip! Is that you?"

Within moments, Owain gently transfers me from his arms into Pip's.

"Oh, my darling, you are safe. I came as soon as I heard what happened."

Smiling weakly, I sit up before I am lifted from the floor. Owain takes my arms, Pip takes my waist and, all the while, Maud still holds my hand.

Sitting on the edge of Lady Stanley's bed, the fog from my mind begins to lift. In front of me, I can see all of the items that Sir William spoke about. They chill me to the bone, especially as the effigy of King Edward is so lifelike. Sickness wells up within my throat as I realise that steel pins have been inserted into King Edward's eye sockets and a blade is lodged within his neck.

Maud, on seeing this, begins to sob loudly. "That's what they did to my husband."

Ned, who had entered without a sound, quickly kneels at Maud's feet, before speaking soft and gentle words, "Please, Lady Willoughby, please let me comfort you."

Quick to accept, she nods and announces that she is to be addressed merely as Maud, then falls into his arms.

Owain, looking incredulously at Ned's cheek, shakes his head, turns and smiles, before addressing Pip. "Pip, do you have word of the cart? Has it been prepared? I'd say that we want to get that witch to Nottingham Castle as soon as possible. News spreads like wildfire and I fear that Lord Stanley will be upon us as soon as he hears what has happened to his wife."

"Ah, fear not, Owain. Lord Stanley and the ringleaders have already been arrested and incarcerated. They languish within the dungeons of Ludlow Castle. I saw to it that a trap was laid on the road from Stratford to Oxford, for if they had made it to Wallingford Castle, they may have found support from Alice Chaucer, the widowed Duchess of Suffolk, who is a most cruel, vindictive, grasping and ruthless woman. The duchess portrays herself nowadays as being a Yorkist, but this has not always been the case, and as I have been unable to ascertain her true loyalties, I am left with no alternative but to strongly suspect that she is still a Lancastrian through and through. Ever since her husband, William de la Pole, who was King Henry VI's favourite, was exiled and beheaded in 1450 after the political violence of the Cade's Revolt, she has been closely entwined with Queen Margaret of Anjou – to the point of being her lady-in-waiting, her friend and her closest confident. I do not like the woman or trust her as far as I can throw her. Our honourable neighbours, the Paston Family, have been hounded by her for years. She is litigious to the extreme and will stop at nothing in the pursuit of advancing her son, John de la Pole, who seeks to reclaim his father's title, the Duke of Suffolk. Alas, she is a member of the Most Noble Order of the Garter and, as such, she tends to get what she wants, but not this time. She has been under constant surveillance for many years, but now that her one-time prisoner and avid supporter, Henry Holland, the Duke of Exeter, has fled into exile in France, where he will eventually join Queen Margaret, she is alone and vulnerable. This means that she is dangerously cornered and has been seeking the support of Sir Thomas Stanley."

Feeling a little better and noticing that I am no longer bleeding, I attempt to stand unassisted. Walking over to the window, I notice that the torches of the Stanley encampment still burn bright as their camp is being dismantled by Sir Allen's men. I long to ask, but dread the answer, so I content myself with the knowledge that the Stanley supporters have most probably been imprisoned for fear that they will start an uprising.

Startled by another knock at the door, I turn to find Morris and Davy standing in the doorway. On seeing my blood-soaked clothing, both are visibly shaken.

Morris, seemingly the worst affected, brushes a tear from his eye. "Mistress Bethany, what has that witch done to you? I will kill her with my own hands for hurting you."

My tears and shock turn to gratefulness and anger. Grateful that I have so many kind people who love and support me, and anger, as that most awful woman could have blinded me or, even worse, killed me.

"I am well, Morris, but I have unfinished business. Will you help me?"

"Why, of course, Mistress, I am always here for you. I always have been, and I always will be. To my dying day."

Drawing strength from deep within, I turn to the room in general and announce that I have unfinished business. "I will not run and hide. Lady Stanley will not leave this place thinking that she has won. Pip, when the cart comes, I want to be the one overseeing her departure."

Pip, knowing my strength of feeling, hesitantly agrees. "Very well, but you are not to go within an arm's length of her."

"Well, that may be difficult for what I have planned. Correct me if I am wrong but shamed women are led half-naked through the streets, aren't they? Surely, as a shamed woman, this should be Lady Stanley's fate?"

Thinking for a moment, Pip begins to nod, as do the others present.

"Lady Maud, will you help me undress Lady Stanley? Her naked shame will be a clear warning to all that see her that those who rise up against King Edward will not go unpunished."

Lady Willoughby rises with intention. "Yes, I will most gladly help you."

"Good. Well, to ensure that we are safe, we will not unchain her. Instead, we will use her scissors to cut her clothing into strips and tear them from her body. Once naked to the waist, we will make her walk to the cart through the castle and the inner bailey. We will also remove her shoes. These will be burned as a symbol." Stopping to think, I ask Pip's advice once more. "Pip, I do not wish Lady Stanley's children to suffer. The faults of their parents are not theirs and they should be spared. Do you agree?"

"Yes, Bethany, I agree. So much so that I have already placed them under the care of Countess Anne Beauchamp, but, Bethany, please tread carefully. Warwick is angered at this arrangement. He is embarrassed and torn by loyalty to both his king and cousin, but also to his sister. Traitor or not, Lady Stanley shares the same blood as him and he will, no doubt, argue that this situation is entirely the fault of Sir Thomas. Who knows what will happen at the trial? Lady Stanley may even be acquitted and sent into exile or honourable imprisonment."

"Yes, Pip, I understand the consequences, but to show weakness now, when everyone present in the great hall witnessed her treasonous words, would probably cause others to think that if she can get away with treason that they can, too."

Nodding, Pip agrees.

Standing at the door of Lady Stanley's chamber, Maud and I hold hands and immediately bond without saying a word. Calling out, I ask Sir William and Sir Allen to unlock the door and admit us, while the others stand guard.

"Please, Sir William, may we have Lady Stanley's small scissors?"

Once provided, Maud and I enter the chamber. It is dimly lit, as even the candles are dying. Approaching the bed, I can immediately see that Lady Stanley does not have a drop of remorse in her eyes. In fact, they are even darker than before. Immediately upon seeing me, her face contorts with anger and her body begins to jolt around uncontrollably. I stop and think. Perhaps cutting her clothes off and shaming her would send the wrong message. To incarcerate her is one thing, but to shame her without a trial would be wrong.

Turning to Maud, I whisper in her ear, "I have decided against my original plan of action. Lady Stanley should be allowed to walk to the cart, with only her hands chained together. We are not in the same vein as this bitter and twisted woman, and however much I wish her to suffer, we will not be her judge and jury. Will you leave with me now and allow the men to escort her to the cart?"

To my surprise, Maud nods her head in agreement. "Yes, Bethany, we will rise above the situation, and we will show mercy – not for her, but for the sake of her children. They may not witness her shame, but one day they will certainly hear of it."

In agreement, we hand the scissors back to Sir William and explain to all that we are retiring to our chambers, before walking away.

We Prepare to Leave

As I wake, I realise that the snow clouds have all disappeared and that the sun is shining. It is a glorious day and, for the first time in weeks, I feel light and unburdened. I am glad that I came to my senses last night and did not allow my anger to overtake my good judgement. My plan to shame Lady Stanley, although justifiable, would have been wrong. She must be treated as innocent until proven guilty, and as an individual, she deserves respect, even if she does not accord others the same courtesy. However, I will think no more of her.

Today is a joyful day! Pip is lying next to me; I can feel his muscular body through his thin linen shift, and I can hear his gentle breathing. I gaze with love upon his face. He is perfect to me. His skin, although weather-beaten from years of campaigning, is unblemished, apart from a faint scar underneath his left eye, which he gained at the first battle of St Albans nearly six years ago. His jaw is strong and angular, and his hair is soft and floppy. Surely he must be aware of my presence as his eyelids have just started to flicker.

"Good morning, my darling Bethany, did you sleep well?"

"Oh yes, far better than I have for months. The wheel of life seems to be turning, and although life will never be the same again, hopefully war will soon be a thing of the past."

Pip agrees. "I would welcome such an outcome. To be free to live the majority of our lives at our manor of South Acre with my mother, brother and Charlemain would please me greatly."

With pleasant thoughts darting around my head, I snuggle into Pip for a few moments longer. Alas, our quiet privacy is soon overtaken by a commotion just beyond the curtains. It sounds like Peter is trying but failing to get Dickon and George to calm down.

"Now listen, boys, your brother, Edward, is on his way and he'll be sorely displeased if you're not dressed and ready to greet him when he arrives."

Far from being concerned, George begins to laugh before answering, "Surely, Peter of Pontefract, we – as princes of the royal blood – have the luxury of being fashionably late."

To this, Dickon can be heard giggling before Peter replies, "Princes of the royal blood, that can't be denied, but fashionably late? You make me laugh. Be careful not to annoy your brother, Prince George, for he has the final say over who your tutor will be, and you wouldn't want to be placed in a household miles from Court or, God forbid, be married within the year to a foreign princess who eats only garlic and snails and runs around trying to kiss you all the time."

A giggling Dickon calls out, "No, brother, that would be even worse than travelling across the country in a hessian bag in the back of a cart."

A laughing George shivers in dramatic fashion. "Yuck! I have no desire to kiss a princess, wherever she comes from."

Pip, looking into my eyes, smiles before saying, "He'll change his mind in a few years, my darling. I was the same at his age, but now I dream of kissing you every single day."

At this, we embrace and kiss one last time, before Pip pulls back the bed curtains and climbs out. "Good morning, all. Peter's right – it's time for us to wash and dress. We must look resplendent today."

With a nod towards a bundle in the corner, Pip asks Peter to fetch the long package. "Now, boys, I want you both to sit on the edge of the bed next to Bethany and be still, for if you don't, you won't get what I've bought for you."

With great excitement, both George and Dickon join me.

Dickon, snuggling into me, asks, "Bethany, please cuddle me. I'm a little nervous about travelling to London, although I know that I shouldn't be."

Putting my arm around Dickon, I realise that I have begun to think of both boys as adopted children. How I long to carry Pip's child and heir.

A smiling Peter bends to pick up the package. I suspect that he is acting, as he is struggling to pick the package up. "Here you go, Pip."

Pip, joining in on the pretence, takes the package and approaches the bed. Both boys being to giggle with excitement. Pip carefully unties the cord before unwrapping the multiple layers of linen. In unison, we all gasp.

"Now, boys, these are blunted and for ceremonial use only, but beware as they can still be used to break bones." We all look on in wonder at the two silver swords, which have been encrusted around the hilt with rubies and sapphires. "Your brother commissioned these for you in recognition of your bravery. He realises just how frightened you both must have been travelling across the country undercover and fearful of being seen."

George stands immediately and asks permission to take one of the swords.

"You do well to ask, George. Your manners will hold you in good stead, as all eyes will be on you both forever more. People not only expect immaculate manners and loyalty from princes of the royal blood, but they also expect you to be brave and honest at all times."

To this, Dickon speaks, "My motto throughout life will be 'Loyalty Binds Me'. I remember Father speaking such words before leaving for Sandal Castle and I will follow his lead in all things. He was a truly great man, wasn't he?"

My eyes fill with tears and I reply, "Yes, Dickon, he was a truly great man."

Pip, managing far better than me to hold back the tears, agrees, "Yes, Dickon, he was a man of strict principles and extreme loyalty. If you follow his example throughout life, you won't go far wrong."

George, far more interested in his sword, is now holding it in both hands and swiping it from side to side.

Sitting comfortably next to Charlemain in the deep window seat and surrounded by cushions, I anticipate King Edward's arrival. Getting ready has taken us hours. Fortunately, Countess Anne sent two of her ladies in waiting and four young pages to assist us, otherwise we still wouldn't be anywhere near ready. With ten of us needing to wash and dress, we required all the help that we could get. Now standing by the fireplace, Alard and Davy are deep in discussion, while Peter and Morris are attempting to lace up

Owain's new tunic. All the while, Ned is playing the fool and blowing on his shawm. Far from being annoyed, it looks like Alard is actually quite pleased for once, as Ned's antics and musical prowess are amusing both George and Dickon.

A knock on the door alerts us to the news that King Edward's baggage train has been sighted and that it is time for us to make our way to the great hall. Jumping into action, the pages and ladies in waiting smooth our Coventry blue cloaks in an attempt to remove as many creases as possible, before draping each one of us in a finely embroidered ceremonial baldrick. The baldricks are spectacular in style and glitter in the sunlight. The design is that of silver and gold ivy, which are entwined with white roses, golden suns and golden crowns.

Looking each one of us up and down, Pip nods his head. "Speaking now as Lord Harsyck, I can say that I am proud of you all. Together, we have defeated an abduction attempt and incarcerated a vicious enemy of the House of York. The future is now looking positive. Once King Edward has been officially crowned, Richard, Duke of York, Richard, Earl of Salisbury and Sir Thomas Neville can be laid to rest, along with all the other Yorkists who sadly lost their lives at the Battles of Wakefield and Towton."

We all cross ourselves, before I put my arms around Dickon's shoulders.

After a respectful silence, Pip continues, "Before we leave this chamber, I have one thing left to do. Bethany, my dearest wife and now an extremely successful Yorkist spy, I have a present for you from the king and I know that he'll expect you to be wearing it when he arrives. Ned, please get that stool from the corner."

Doing as he is told, Ned retrieves the stool and places it just behind me. "Bethany, please be seated, shut your eyes and do not open them until the time is right."

Confused by such a strange request, I look up into Pip's eyes and enquire, "You say when the time is right, but how will I know when that is?"

Morris begins to laugh. "Oh, you'll know alright, trust me."

Fascinated and confused, I shut my eyes as tight as possible, screwing them up until I feel the skin on my face tighten. I then hear the door open and someone enter, before the words, "Oh no, I never realised that you would be here, you old codger!"

To this, we all laugh. I spin around and stand immediately. "Alice, how lovely to see you!"

Taking my hands, Alice smiles before hugging me. "Oh, Mistress Bethany, I have missed you."

Hugging Alice tight, I express how much I have missed her, too.

Morris, sensing an opportunity to wind Alice up, says, "Well, that's enough of that. You're here to work, Alice. Do you remember what that is?"

Alice immediately releases me and turns to Morris. "Now, you can stop your beefing. Of course I know what work is." Laughter fills the air and immediately Alice realises that Morris has been goading her. "You old goat, you. I'll get my own back when the time is right, but for now, I have work to do, so stop holding me up."

With this, Alice removes my coif and begins to brush my hair, before pulling a section of it into a tight topknot and securing it with pins. "Ah, that should hold nicely. Now, Lord Philip, please pass me King Edward's gift."

Pip turns and picks up a beautifully carved wooden box. "Here you go, Bethany. This is for you."

I take the box and examine it carefully before opening it. The box is long and narrow and not overly deep – probably about two hands deep. I wonder what on earth it could be. My hands tremble with excitement. In the middle of the lid, my initials have been engraved in an elaborate style. Above my initials are two crests. One belonging to the Harsyck family and the other belonging to the Mortimer family. Below this is a single Yorkist rose and a sun. I run my fingers over the carvings and contemplate the work that has gone into this gift, before unlatching the clasp and opening the lid. I gasp in delight when I see a fine white hennin and matching veil. I have seen fine ladies wearing these conical style headdresses and veils before, but never in my wildest dreams could I ever have imagined that I would wear one, let alone own one, as they are usually worn by princesses or important women at court. I remove it and turn it this way and that before handing it to Alice.

"What a beauty! Now, please sit very still, Mistress, as I need to position this over the topknot and pin it securely in place. We don't want it to move when travelling now, do we?"

Once Alice is content, I carefully unwrap the linen and remove the veil. Stunned by its beauty, I gaze upon the embossed white roses that follow the lower hem. Unable to speak, I pass the veil to Alice.

"Thank you, Mistress. This is the easy part. I just need to ensure that the veil is correctly attached to your hair and the base of the hennin."

Looking around the room, I notice that everyone is watching intently and smiling back at me.

Ready at last, we all stand. Once everyone is in position, I make my way to the door where I am joined by Charlemain, who offers me his arm.

"Oh, Mistress, how far we have come in just a few years. You are a credit to my family and greatly loved by everyone. It is now protocol that we must lead up our retinue and accompany both young George and Dickon, who we must now address as princes."

Looking at them both, my heart fills with joy. I smile, nod and happily agree. We leave the chamber, two by two, and head for the inner courtyard.

The Arrival of Glorious King Edward

Standing proudly within the inner courtyard and awaiting the imminent arrival of King Edward, I am surrounded by the Harsyck retinue. We look a sight to behold in our finery. My heart is light and I feel full of joy, as Sir William has just informed us that the plot to abduct both Dickon and George has failed in its entirety, and Lord Stanley and his inner circle of supporters have all been arrested. A trial will now be scheduled and their fate will be decided by a jury. I am glad that Lady Willoughby and myself rose above our anger and that we did not humiliate Lady Stanley. She, no doubt, will humiliate herself. However, I feel pity for her children, who now stand alongside the Countess Anne and her family.

There are gasps all around as King Edward enters through the magnificent archway. Shining like the sun, he looks utterly magnificent in a heavily padded gambeson, which is emblazoned with both his and the full Mortimer coat of arms. On one sleeve, his livery badge, the Sun in Splendour, is surrounded by individual golden suns, while on the other sleeve are training white roses. Bringing his black horse to a halt, he catapults himself to a standing position just in front of Warwick.

Warwick immediately steps forward and kneels in deference, before beginning, "Welcome, cousin. Glorious King Edward IV of England. I kneel here as your humble servant, ready to make you the finest king in all of Christendom."

Edward learns forward and responds quietly, with a gentle annoyance in his voice, "You are mistaken, cousin. My father ensured that his rightful heirs would be the finest kings in the whole of Christendom when he rightfully laid claim to the throne of England less than a year ago. He fought for his rights and the rights of his sons on that day in October, when all you could do was to argue in private that he should not have acted without consulting either you or your father. No, Warwick, you are not in charge. In fact, if you don't begin to demonstrate your complete and utter loyalty to me very soon, you may well end up on a charge. Charged with treason, in the same vein as your sister – that black-hearted wife of Stanley, who, as we speak, is incarcerated within the deepest dungeon at Nottingham Castle under my direct orders. A place where her husband and his supporters will soon join her. I have directed that they be given a fair trial, but I have also been clear in my instructions that treason is punishable by death. You would do well to remember that – especially as I see and hear everything that goes on and I am more that capable of dealing with every situation myself. I do not need you; you need me. For without my patronage, your fiefdom would come tumbling down around you. For it is within my power to seize all that you have and to either keep it for myself or to give it away to those who are loyal to me. Just remember that, cousin."

Standing upright once more and smiling, Edward leaves Warwick kneeling in a state of shock, with a face as white as snow. However, Warwick soon regains his composure and stands before bowing low. "Cousin, I pledge my complete allegiance and my unwavering support."

Edward just smiles and walks off towards the Countess Anne and her children. At the top of the steps, leading to the great hall, it is obvious that the excitement is just too much to bear for Isabel and Anne, who are desperately trying to escape their mother's grasp, for they pull and sway from side to side. Edward, noting this immediately, kneels on the spot. A smiling Anne then lets her hands fall away from theirs and they run towards Edward. Flinging their arms around him, they hug him tightly and smother him with kisses. Standing, he lifts both girls. One in either arm.

"Now, that's the welcome that I expected." Laughing, he lowers them to the ground. However, they still cling onto him.

Margaret, being that touch older, smiles shyly before lowering into a deep curtsy. Edward, intent on making Margaret break her demeanour, asks, "Is that all that I get now that I am king?"

Margaret, immediately pushing the official protocol to one side, rises and runs into Edward's open arms. A laughing Edward says, "That's more like it. I am surrounded by three beautiful young ladies." To this everyone laughs and we all file into the hall.

Inside, pages circulate and ask that we take our seats and await the arrival of the refreshments. However, Edward, who has just seen Lady Willoughby standing to one side, immediately approaches her and kisses her on both cheeks.

"My dearest Maud, how I have longed to see you. We have endured the greatest pain since Wakefield and I know that your heart is broken and that it will be for many years to come – maybe forever. However, there is one close by who I know has a kindling of love for you. One that I approve of wholeheartedly and one who I suspect would heal your pain. I beseech you to keep an open heart and try to live again. For I know that Thomas loved you so much that it would break his heart to see you in such a state. He would want you to pick up the pieces that are left behind and live with happiness and remembrance in your heart."

Maud smiles weakly. "I cannot promise, but I will try to open my heart and see what happens. Although, I tell you truthfully, that I have wished myself dead since the Battle of Wakefield. The pain is almost too much to bear."

With a forlorn look, Edward agrees. "Yes, the pain of loss is unbearable." Leading Maud by the hand, he invites her to sit beside him.

Once we are all seated and comfortable, innumerable dishes are served from the kitchen to which Edward begins to laugh. "Cousin, I said light refreshments before we leave."

Warwick, appearing back to normal, laughs. "Well, we have plenty of rooms prepared should the need arise."

After eating, a single harpist begins to play as the tables are being cleared. King Edward stands and stretches before addressing the great hall.

"Before we leave, I have something very important that

I must do. There are many in this room who I would like to honour for their loyal service to me." With this, Edward's page approaches the dais and carefully hands Edward a large red velvet cushion, which is edged with golden braid, before bowing and backing away. Edward, obviously pleased with his page, smiles. "Now, when I call your name, please come forward and stand in a line."

Pride swells inside me as Pip, Alard, Owain, Davy, Morris, Peter, Charlemain, Sir Allen and Sir William are all called forward. However, we are all horrified when Ned's name is not called. Unable to say anything, Pip and the others follow Edward's command.

"Please hold out your hands and receive these golden livery badges with my heartfelt thanks for your loyalty. I owe you all so much more than a piece of gold and be assured that I will do everything that I can to look after you and yours forever more."

Gratefully, each man receives and pins their badges to their cloaks.

"These golden suns will tell all who see them that you are my men. Men so valued that I choose you above all others."

Returning to Ned's side, I see the sadness in their eyes. I ask myself, *Why?* Why has Edward chosen to leave Ned out? Ned is as true and loyal as the others. I just don't understand. In shocked amazement, I look at Edward and realise that he is smiling at everyone's discomfort.

"Now, why all the glum faces? Surely you should all be rejoicing. Have I not honoured you all?"

I can see that Pip longs to speak, but that he will not do so unless invited by Edward, for Edward is the king and lower mortals have no right to question the king's actions.

"Have I forgotten someone? Surely not. I never forget anything or anyone."

Pip, still longing to speak, remains quiet but makes an exaggerated glance in Ned's direction.

Edward, seeing this, laughs. "Fear not, my loyal friends, for I have not forgotten Ned. How could I? That awful shawm and the chaos that ensues wherever he goes. How could I ever forget Ned." I breathe a silent sigh of relief. "Ned, I have something extremely special for you. Come forward and kneel before me."

Ned bounds forward and kneels, as Edward walks back to his chair and unsheathes his sword. Holding it high in the air, Edward turns it around and around in his hands before returning to Ned.

"Ned, I have something of far greater value and far greater beauty than gold to give to you. For your many years of service to me and my father, I would like to knight you."

At this, Ned falters and momentarily falls backwards, before righting himself.

"Once you are a knight, you will be able to marry the bride of your choice, if she agrees, and I suspect that there is one in this room who you would like to love and protect forever. Am I right?"

Ned, for once speechless, blushes and nods in agreement.

Edward turns and smiles towards Lady Willoughby, who carefully removes her black lace veil and smiles. Turning back to Ned, Edward proceeds, "Ned, all formalities will be completed on the eve of my coronation, but in the meantime I use my sword to dub you a knight and hereby grant you the manor of West Acre. By granting you this manor, I command that you remain in the service of my most trusted knight, Lord Philip Harsyck, and that you use all available funds to support your future wife, when the time comes. Arise, Sir Edward, Lord of West Acre."

Ned stands and the great hall erupts with joy. The cheering is almost deafening. Bowing low before Edward, I can see Ned silently thanking Edward before retrieving his shawm and dancing over to Lady Willoughby. Kneeling before Maud, Ned can be seen to exchange a few silent words to her, before kissing her outstretched hand.

However, it would seem that King Edward is not finished just yet. To my surprise, he is beckoning me forward. "Lady Phillip Harsyck, Bethany Mortimer, please step forward, I have a gift for you."

Immediately alarmed, I touch my hennin and veil. Surely I have already received my gifts.

"I see that you touch my earlier gifts. They suit you, but your hennin appears to be missing a crucial component."

I look towards Pip and then Alice and note confusion on their faces.

"Please kneel before me."

I do as Edward commands. Smiling, he turns and picks up a small linen bag. He puts his hand in the bag and pretends to fumble around, before pulling from within a small golden circlet – the beauty of which catches my breath and that of others close by.

"Please accept this circlet for your bravery and loyalty to me and my father. You have carried out your duties admirably. Please wear it with pride, when the occasion allows. The enamelled white roses and the golden suns will tell all who cast eyes upon it where your loyalties lie."

Unable to stop myself, tears spill from my eyes before Edward takes my hand and helps me to my feet. "Alice, we must leave shortly, therefore please approach and set Bethany's circlet in place with pins, but before you do, I have a present for you."

Alice, never one to be quiet, is for once stunned into silence.

"Come forward, but do not kneel." Delving into the linen bag once more, Edward presents Alice with a pair of beautifully decorated scissors and a golden thimble.

Alice, still lost for words, bows her head and stands completely still until a voice calls out, "Come on Alice! It'll be nightfall before we know it."

To this everyone laughs, even Alice.

Outside, Edward mounts his horse and calls forward his retinue, behind which Morris manoeuvres Liege and Freemantle. As I climb into the cart, I notice that Morris is holding a set of brand-new red leather reins in his old hands.

"These were a present to Liege and Fremantle from King Edward. He has a good heart that one. His father would be proud of him."

Agreeing wholeheartedly, I take up my seat in the back of the cart and hold out my hand to Lady Willoughby, who joins me. Still smiling from ear to ear, Maud has the look of one who has just found love.

"Oh Bethany, is this real or am I dreaming?"

"Maud, this is real. Ned's love for you is clear for all to see, and our friendship will never be broken."

Morris, clearly touched by recent events, calls out to Charlemain, "Come on Charlemain! Get in the cart. You're almost as bad as Alice for timekeeping."

Laughter rings out once more.

"I'll be with you in just a moment, Morris. I just need to make sure that the princes are mounted safely and that their horses tack is in place, then we'll be on our way."

At this, Sir William and Sir Allen's men form a guard of honour, as Countess Anne's cart draws up behind us and a mounted Warwick takes up the flank with his retinue. Safe in the knowledge that we are protected, Maud and I relax and wait patiently until Charlemain and Alice climb aboard.

King Edward, sensing that everybody is now in place, turns and looks over his right shoulder. The pride on his face is unmissable. With all three brothers mounted, King Edward announces, "Well, if everyone is ready, it is time for us to leave. We are set for London and the greatest coronation of all time. The Sun in Splendour will shine forever more!"